WITHDRAWN

D1058771

Die for You

ALSO BY AMY FELLNER DOMINY

A Matter of Heart

OyMG

Audition & Subtraction

Die for You

AMY
FELLNER
DOMINY

DELACORTE PRESS

Text copyright © 2016 by Amy Fellner Dominy
Jacket art copyright © 2016 by Vanesa Munoz / Trevillion Images
Jacket design by Laura Klynstra

All rights reserved. Published in the United States by Delacorte Press,
an imprint of Random House Children's Books,
a division of Penguin Random House LLC, New York.

Delacorte Press is a registered trademark and the colophon
is a trademark of Penguin Random House LLC.

randomhouseteens.com

Educators and librarians, for a variety of teaching tools, visit us at
RHTeachersLibrarians.com

Library of Congress Cataloging-in-Publication Data
Names: Dominy, Amy Fellner, author.
Title: Die for you / Amy Fellner Dominy.
Description: First Edition. | New York : Delacorte Press, [2016]
Summary: Eighteen-year-old Emma Lorde thought her gorgeous, good guy
boyfriend, Dillon, had saved her life, but senior year has brought about
many changes and challenges to their picture perfect future.
Identifiers: LCCN 2015034488 | ISBN 978-1-101-93619-1 (hc) |
ISBN 978-1-101-93621-4 (ebook)
Subjects: | CYAC: Love—Fiction.
Classification: LCC PZ7.D71184 Di 2016 | DDC [Fic]—dc23

The text of this book is set in 12-point Jenson Pro.
Interior design by Trish Parcell

Printed in the United States of America
10 9 8 7 6 5 4 3 2 1
First Edition

For my daughter, Rachel

THE SERPENT RING

By Emma Lorde

AUGUST 24, AD 79

SECOND HOUR, 8:00 A.M.

On the day before the world explodes, Anna wakes in the bustling city of Pompeii to the feel of the earth moving beneath her.

Another tremor, she thinks. This one is long and shuddering, as if the earth is also waking up. The tremors have been growing steadily over the past months. Just yesterday in the market, the ground shook so hard she nearly fell. Marcus was there. He'd steadied Anna with his hand on her arm. She trembled then, didn't she?

Marcus is the son of a patrician and she a slave, but he doesn't touch her like a slave. Each day he buys his lunch at the thermopolium where she works. Each day he looks at her as if he wants more than what she serves from the heated terra-cotta pots. He has grown bolder in recent weeks. Whispered words of admiration have turned to promises of love. She is not free,

1

she reminds him, and he bristles at that. He will speak to his father. He will buy her freedom. He is so bold. Strong. Gods be good, she has begun to hope.

And so she waits for the start of her new life. Will today be the day?

Beneath her feet, the ground shakes again. It is the day before a never-ending night, and Anna feels only the beat of her heart.

1

"Watch out," Hannah says. "There's a sweaty guy headed your way."

I follow her gaze to the baseball diamond and laugh as Dillon hops the low fence surrounding the field and jogs toward the bleachers where Hannah and I are still sitting, along with most of the parents. The team won in the bottom of the ninth, and we're basking in the victory. My throat aches from screaming. I've become one of those girls who jump up and down and shrieks like a game of baseball is the most important thing in the world.

Of course it's not.

Dillon Hobbs, on the other hand . . .

He sees me watching and grins. I know that grin.

"Don't you dare!" I call.

It's only the second week of March, but summer likes to come early in Phoenix and it's in the mid-nineties today. Dillon's been strapped into his catcher's gear for nine innings,

3

except for when he was sprinting to the bases and diving headfirst to beat out a tag. His gold jersey is soaked with sweat, plastered to his wide shoulders and the flat ridges of his abs. His black hair is just as wet—slicked back and dripping with the remains of a jug of Gatorade dumped over him after his bloop single brought in the winning run and clinched a win against our biggest rivals.

When his cleats hit the metal ramp, their clatter is drowned out as the parents stand and cheer, then make a path for him.

He takes the steps two at a time, shaking off droplets of liquid like a wet dog. A very dirty wet dog. Dust is smeared across his forehead, and his dark maroon socks are caked brown with the same mud that covers his white pants. There's a chorus of laughter as I grab Hannah's shoulder and climb up a row, putting her in front of me like a human shield.

"Come on," he says, stopping just below Hannah. "We just beat Hampton. I need a hug." He holds out his grimy arms.

"I'm embracing you from afar," I say from behind Hannah. "And later I'm going to embrace the showered and sweat-free you."

His grin widens.

Hannah shifts out of the way. "You've got to take one for the team, Emma."

There's more laughter as she shares a high five with Dillon.

"Traitor," I say.

"Give up," he intones in a deep and oh-so-sexy voice. "There's no escape."

And then he leaps up the row, grabs me in his arms, and lifts me against him. Sweat and mud and smelly boy press against me from head to toe. I groan at the death of my white

T-shirt as more laughter rings out. And then I hug him back. I can't help but smile.

It's good to see him happy like this.

Dillon has been struggling since we started back after winter break, wound tighter and tighter as we go from one *last* to another. Last baseball season. Last Valentine's dance. Last spring break. Graduation is weighing on everyone, but on Dillon most of all. So I love it when he loses himself in the moment, like now.

It's a perfect afternoon. Nothing but clear skies and cotton-ball clouds. Spring break is officially here, and the Ridgeway baseball team is off to a winning start. Small things, yeah, but I've come to appreciate those in the past year.

"We're going to celebrate at Pizza Joe's," Dillon says. "Jace, Spence . . . I'm sure Hannah, too. You're coming, right?"

I glance over at the fence. Hannah has found her way down to Spence. They're nearly the same height, both with honey-blond hair, and could pass as brother and sister. Which would be creepy seeing as how they're officially an item now. Dillon's closest friend, Jace, who's next to them, is usually a head above everyone else, but he's bent over tugging off the ankle brace he's been wearing this spring.

The four of them have been best friends since elementary school and I try not to feel like a fifth wheel. Mostly they've been great—treating me like one of the group. They did it for Dillon at first, but more and more I feel like they're my friends now, too. Still, there are times when I look at how close they are and I miss Marissa. She's my history, the best friend I left behind when I moved across town last May. Marissa and I try to stay close, but it's hard when we live so far apart.

5

"I'll try," I say. "I've got to meet Mrs. Lyght, remember?"

"I forgot," he says.

He lets go and I look down at myself. "I've been slimed."

Dillon's dark eyes skim over my chest and then lower. His lips part and his eyes narrow in a look that still takes my breath away. "You look good slimed."

Warmth shivers through me. "Later," I say. "I have a meeting."

He brushes a chunk of mud off my shoulder. "Love you, Emma Lorde."

"I love you, too, Dillon Hobbs. Now go away." With a laugh, I push his soggy chest with the flat of my palm. "I have to clean up—somehow."

"I'll see you later, then." He kisses me and I taste the grit of dirt and sweat and lemon Gatorade. I smile. If forever had a flavor, this would be it.

2

"How would you like to spend next year in Rome?"

I stare at Mrs. Lyght. I'm suddenly having a difficult time processing the English language.

"Ummmm?" It sounds like a question. I cover my mouth with my hand, but other words don't appear to be coming out any time soon.

The classroom is awkwardly quiet. Even the air conditioner has kicked off, and I wonder if it's already shut down for spring break. I should be gone, too, having pizza with Dillon, Jace, Spence, and Hannah. But I'm here, my white shirt still wet and stained in splotches, as if I've had a run-in with a used tea bag.

I figured Mrs. Lyght wanted to meet with me to talk about my dad's summer program. He teaches archaeology at Arizona State University, and every year he arranges expeditions for his grad students. Mrs. Lyght is usually one of his teaching assistants. It was actually one of the nicest surprises I got when I transferred to Ridgeway for my senior year—a history teacher I already knew. But it also means I have to tiptoe around why Dad hasn't planned anything for this summer. When she asks, I'll blame it on the divorce and the move. *He wanted to stick around—for my sake.* It sounds so much better than the truth.

But that's not what she's asking.

I clear my throat. "Rome, Italy?" I say.

"That would be the one." The history teacher at my last school was a human artifact, but Mrs. Lyght is still young enough to pull off squared black glasses and short hair the color of a penny. Her smile widens and I wonder if she can tell my heart is racing and fireworks are going off inside my head. *Rome, Italy—City of the Seven Hills. City of the Great Empire. City of Love. City of my dreams.*

"I have an opportunity for you, Emma." She rests her elbows on the desk. A paper crumbles beneath her and she brushes it out of the way. "A friend of mine runs a small museum in Rome. Each year, he brings in a study-abroad student to work there. He was just told that the person he had lined up has to drop out. His second and third choices have already committed elsewhere, so now he's scrambling. There's just not enough time to start the application process again. He asked me and a few other colleagues if we had any students we could recommend."

My heart drops like a yo-yo, then shoots up again. "Me?"

"If you're interested."

"If I'm interested?" The expression *I'd give my right nut* pops into my head. What's the female version, I wonder? And

8

why am I thinking about this right now while Mrs. Lyght is staring at me like she might be reconsidering?

"Of course I'm interested," I say quickly. "I just can't take it all in. I mean, *Rome*. It's always been a dream of mine."

It's embarrassing to admit, but my fascination with Rome started with the movie *Gladiator*. All the blood and guts grossed me out but at the same time, I couldn't get over the fact that Rome was the center of art and culture. How could one society have so much destruction *and* creation?

By then I knew I wanted to be an archaeologist like Dad, but that's when I first started obsessing about all things Roman. Then Dad bought me a book about Pompeii, and I just *knew*. Dad says it happens that way for a lot of archaeologists. They connect to some particular time or place and that becomes their focus—often for their whole careers. As soon as I saw the pictures and read the stories, I knew where I wanted to work.

There's just nothing like Pompeii. Only a few hours from Rome, it's an entire city perfectly preserved under fourteen feet of volcanic ash. You can see the homes, gardens, bathhouses, and art. They've made casts of the bodies exactly how they were found, and they're so detailed you can read the expressions on the townspeople's faces.

Over the years, I've read so much about Pompeii I sometimes wake up hearing the screams of the people and tasting volcanic ash in my throat. To think that I could actually visit and maybe even volunteer makes my fingers itch. The collection of broken pottery and colored tile must be incredible. Pieces of the past waiting to be made whole. It's what

I'm good at, what I love most—fitting together jagged bits of pottery. Dad says it's a gift I have, like a sculptor who can see a statue in a block of stone. I can picture the original shape of an artifact from just a few pieces, sense the patterns and designs before other people can. It's the most amazing feeling in the world, too, when you put something back together— turn rubble into real.

My thoughts rush ahead. From what I've read, Pompeii is just a train ride from Rome. If I lived in the city, I could go anytime I wanted. I shiver at the thought. Traveling abroad was a dream I buried when Mom and Dad fell apart. It was all I could do to hold things together here. But now . . . I feel like Mrs. Lyght has dug up those dreams.

She leans forward, and my attention shifts back to her. "Tell me what you're thinking."

I run my palms over my jean shorts. My hands feel damp with sweat while my legs are shaky with goose bumps. "Just about all the things I've read but have never seen. Rome . . . Pompeii."

She nods. "It's one of the reasons why I thought of you for this opportunity. Your project last semester on culture in Pompeii was excellent. College level."

I smile, feeling as if I might float out of my chair. "They're still getting packages in the mail at Pompeii," I say. "Did you know that? People who have stolen bits of glass or tile are sending them back. Some of them from fifty years ago."

Mrs. Lyght raises her eyebrows. "That would make working in the mailroom an interesting job."

"Scrubbing toilets would be an interesting job if it was in Pompeii."

She laughs. "So you like the idea of a year in Italy?"

"Are you kidding? What do I do? How can I make it happen?"

"First things first," Mrs. Lyght says. "You need to talk it over with your parents. They'll want to be part of the decision."

"Oh, sure. I will." I nod as if my parents are part of any of my decisions these days.

"The internship only pays a small stipend, but you will earn credits through the American University of Rome. You'll have to look into registration beginning with the fall semester."

"I can figure it out over spring break."

"Good," she says. "Use the week to think it over. If you still feel certain this is something you want, then come see me a week from Monday and you'll get your assignment."

"Assignment?"

"You won't be the only student considered. In order to be chosen, you'll have to impress Dr. Abella with your abilities to handle the job."

"Abilities?" I feel like a not-very-bright parrot.

"He'll need someone with basic research skills, general education, and some experience with artifacts," she explains. "I imagine you'll be competing mainly against college students, but you've had very unique opportunities because of your father. I think you have a good chance."

"Can I get the assignment now?"

She smiles. "Take the week, Emma. Let the idea settle. It's a big commitment and it would mean a lot of changes."

"But . . . Rome?"

She pulls off her glasses and laughs. "Yes, Rome."

It's possible I walk to the door, but I have no memory of moving my feet. I'm weightless. I feel like too much blood has gone to my head and not enough oxygen to my lungs.

Somehow, I'm outside. Fresh air hits my face and life suddenly rushes back at me as if I'd hit the pause button while I was inside.

Oh God.

Dillon.

3

"No way," Dillon says, pointing a finger at me in warning.

"Just try it," I say. I leverage myself higher on his chest and wiggle a Raisinet near his lips. "Come on."

He's lying back, head propped up on two pillows, his bare chest damp and bathed in candlelight. His skin smells good—a mix of his ocean-fresh body spray and us. The sheet is tangled around our legs and our legs are tangled around each other. I love these moments after. The guesthouse silent around us, the rest of the world a million miles away. It's just the two of us . . . and Dillon's secret stash of candy.

Dillon is one of those annoyingly healthy people who don't just talk about eating right; he actually does it. Except for his one vice, candy, and not just any kind—Junior Mints. It's become a challenge to get him to try something different.

"This could be your new favorite," I say. "Chocolate. Fruit. What's not to love?"

He fishes a Junior Mint out of his box. "I know what I like.

Why mess with perfection?" His gaze drops to the curve of my breasts and his lips part in a slow smile. He slides the mint in my mouth. I roll the chocolate around and let the icy center melt on my tongue.

"Mmm," he says in a low voice. "Do that again."

I shake my head. "Your turn." I dance the Raisinet across the smoothness of his chest. "Come on. I tried yours. You try mine."

He stares at the brown blob in my fingers and makes the sign of the cross.

I laugh. "You're such a candy snob."

"I am not. I've been known to have the occasional M&M. But as the former owner of a rabbit, I can never eat a Raisinet."

"You had a rabbit?"

"Mr. Big Ears. He pooped Raisinets all day long."

"It's chocolate."

"It's chocolate-covered rabbit poop."

"What if my life was at stake?" I demand. "And the only way to save me was to eat a Raisinet?"

He blinks sadly as he slides his hand down my side and squeezes my butt. "I'll miss you."

I gasp in mock horror. "That's it," I say. "You are going to eat this."

His eyes glitter black in the dim light. "Never."

I raise my eyebrows and slide up his body, trailing one hand along his thigh. His body stiffens and a spark flares in his midnight-blue eyes.

I kiss the fullness of his bottom lip and then twist so I'm lying beside him, my head on my pillow. I set the Raisinet inside my belly button.

He groans. "That's not fair." He rises onto one elbow, his black hair falling over his forehead. He kisses my shoulder and then the hollow between my breasts. His head drops and my breath catches. I feel his tongue dip into my navel, and then he looks up, the Raisinet in his teeth.

He bites down on it and a look of horror paints his face. His lips pucker. He's like a five-year-old trying Brussels sprouts for the first time. "That's awful!"

I burst out laughing as he buries his head in my stomach. He wraps his arms around me and we lie like that, shaking enough to make the mattress squeak until our laughter fades into a sigh.

"I don't want to go," he says into my ribs. "A week is too long."

"I'm the one who's going to be miserable. You'll be on a cruise, distracted by all the girls in bikinis."

"I don't even see other girls. Don't you know that by now?" He looks up, the candle flickering warm light on one smooth cheek, the straight slope of his nose, the barest trace of stubble that grows in patches along his jaw. "I wish you were coming with me."

"Even if your mom wanted me along, I'm meeting my sister early tomorrow."

He slides up beside me and squeezes my shoulder. He knows it's going to be a hard morning. Lauren is driving up from the University of Arizona and we're going to meet at Mom's to pack up her old bedroom. But really it's a last good-bye to the house we grew up in.

"I hate that I won't be here for you."

I press a kiss on the curve of his collarbone. "I'll be okay.

I'll have Lauren there, and then I'm going to hang out with Marissa."

"I won't even be able to call."

"I'm trying not to think about that."

His chest rises and then falls with a long exhale. "I don't think we've ever gone more than a day without talking."

I smile, thinking of all the times my phone buzzed with one of Dillon's late-night calls. Usually it was just a quick good night. A sleepy, "I love you, Em." And then there were the nights when I couldn't sleep and I'd call him and say, "Watch a show with me?" And he'd turn on his TV and I'd turn on mine and we'd watch the same show, not talking but just feeling—needing—the connection.

"I'm going to miss you so much, Em," he murmurs.

I tense. It's been such a wonderful night. I haven't wanted to spoil it with Rome, but now his words remind me. I have to tell him.

Just a few minutes more . . .

He shifts and pulls me onto his chest. I sigh into the ridge of muscle beneath my cheek. I can hear the steady beat of his heart, slow now and strong, like everything about Dillon. He isn't much taller than I am, but he's solid muscle everywhere. He pushes my hair back behind my ear, trailing a finger over the sapphire earring he gave me at Christmas. "She thinks it'll be good for us. She told me that yesterday."

I don't have to ask who. Dillon's mom has wanted us to take a break ever since he brought me home to meet her last June. I glance toward the window as if I'll see her standing there. But it's dark outside; even the landscape lights in Dillon's backyard have clicked off, which they do every night at eleven-thirty. The guesthouse is tucked in the back corner of his yard, surrounded by trees that block most of the view from the two-story house. She never comes out, never checks up on Dillon, but I see the blinds move sometimes and I know she's there. There's something a little creepy about how much she watches over him, but Dillon is all she's got now. And he's careful of her feelings. How can I fault him for that—it's one of the things I most admire about Dillon. He takes care of the people he loves.

"She's afraid of losing you," I murmur. Even though she won't.

Dillon and I are both registered at ASU next year. We're going to live in the dorms, so he'll only be ten miles away. I know she was hoping he'd stay in the guesthouse, but he's promised he'll come home some weekends and live here over summer breaks. He almost lives here now.

Dillon used to have trouble sleeping. He says he's always been a night owl, but Jace, who's known him longer than anyone, told me it got worse after Dillon's dad died three years ago. That's when he started going for late-night runs, but that scared Mrs. Hobbs, so they came up with this—a gym in the guesthouse. She bought Dillon a weight bench and a treadmill with a TV mounted to the wall. When he got restless at night, he could work out and run until he got tired. Of course, I didn't know any of this when we started dating. Not until one hot night in June when we were watching a movie in the guesthouse and he fell asleep.

We'd been officially dating for four weeks, but he'd never drifted off like that before, even though he spent long hours in the sun as a lifeguard. I remember watching him sleep, how everything about him seemed perfect to me. The slight wing of his eyebrows. The way his spiky black lashes curled the tiniest bit at the tip. The feel of his calloused fingers laced through mine. Even asleep—with his breathing deep and regular—he still held my hand. I wanted to freeze time so the moment would never end, but Dad was still drinking too much then and I really needed to get home. I turned off the TV and slowly wiggled my fingers free. When I did, he woke up.

"I have to leave," I whispered. "Go back to sleep."

He blinked dazedly. "I fell asleep?"

"It's okay. It's late, and the movie was terrible."

"No," he murmured. "You don't understand."

I thought he must be embarrassed that he'd dozed off, but his lips parted in a sweet grin—a boyishly beautiful grin. He found my fingers again, wrapping them in his. "I never fall sleep like this."

"Like what?"

"Like . . . peacefully."

I blushed, ridiculously happy. I felt like I'd just discovered a superpower. My lips still fighting a smile, I pressed a kiss to the corner of his mouth. "I have to go."

He squeezed my fingers tighter. "What if I don't ever want you to go?"

There was something new in his voice. Something that made my heart flutter at the base of my throat. "That would be okay with me."

His voice was rough with sleep and some deeper emotion. "Be my girlfriend, Em? I feel like you already are."

I nodded, the blood fizzing in my veins as I looked at our clasped hands. "I feel that way, too."

He lifted my hand to his face and rubbed his cheek in my palm. "I was dreaming about you," he said.

"You were?"

He nodded as his eyes lifted to mine, the hypnotic blue of deep waters. "I think I have been my whole life."

He started sleeping better after that but he didn't tell his mom. He had other reasons now for wanting the privacy of the guesthouse. It's a nice place, and we're lucky to have it, but it also makes me feel claustrophobic. I glance toward the living room curtains I can't see except in my mind.

The light from the clock catches my eye. It's nearly midnight. Dad will be asleep, but I really should go. I have to tell Dillon. He'll be upset at first, but all afternoon I've been imagining us together in Rome over the holidays and now it feels real. If I can just paint the picture for him . . .

I pull the sheet with me as I scoot up straighter and sit back against the pillow. "So I never told you about my meeting with Mrs. Lyght."

"I thought it was something to do with your dad?"

"Not exactly."

His eyes watch me, a line just visible between his brows.

"It turns out Mrs. Lyght has a friend who runs a museum. He has a grant to bring in an intern every year and the person he had lined up for next year just bailed. He needs someone else but doesn't have time to go through the application process. He asked Mrs. Lyght if she had any students to recommend."

19

"She recommended you?"

"I still have to apply," I say. "But . . ."

He tucks a lock of hair behind my ear. "But you're amazing."

"Here's the amazing part." I pause. "The museum is in Rome."

"Italy?" He stiffens, the muscles in his arms flexing.

"I know. I can hardly believe it myself."

"For the summer?" He goes still. It's not as if he was moving before, but something about him coils as tight as a rattlesnake. It's how Dillon absorbs bad news. As if he's steadying himself.

But this isn't bad news.

I work to keep the smile on my lips as my hands press the sheet to my chest. I can feel my heart thumping. "The year," I say. "I'd leave in August, come home in May. But you'll come out for the holidays. Just think about it, Dillon. Christmas in Rome. We'll watch the sun set over St. Peter's Basilica. Who knows. Maybe the pope will be in residence." I smile wider, wanting to make him smile, too. "And we'll sit at little cafes and eat pasta and drink Italian wine."

It's like he doesn't hear any of that. "The *year*?" he repeats. A nerve twitches by the side of his eye and a strange look transforms his features into someone I hardly recognize. I've seen flashes of it this spring—almost a look of panic, as though he's just realized his wallet is missing.

I shift uneasily. It's his fear of everything changing—that's what's thrown him off. Dillon arranges his life the same way he's arranged his collection of miniature cars. Each one is in a special place. One time I picked up a car and he took it from me before I could put it back, carefully setting it in the exact same spot, at the exact same angle. He's like that during a baseball game, too, always signaling the number of outs, pointing to the fielder where he expects the ball to be hit, calling each pitch of the game. It's his way of controlling a world that felt beyond his control growing up. I get that. But now his friends are splintering off. Spence is going to San Diego for college, and lately Jace—his closest friend since fourth grade—is acting strange whenever next year comes up, as though he's changed his mind about ASU. I don't want Dillon to think I'm a splinter, too.

"The time would go fast," I say. "You'll be busy with classes, and we can Skype every day."

"But you're already registered for ASU. We're applying for the same dorm. You wouldn't . . . you . . . you're not really . . ." He licks his lips, and I know he's waiting. *For what? For me to make this all go away?*

I feel like there's a fist in my throat. It's hard to breathe. "I know there's a lot to figure out." I find myself talking faster, covering up his silence. "I'm not sure, but I think I'd get transfer credits. I'd attend a university in Rome, and probably take classes in the mornings and work at the museum in the afternoons. Think how much I'd learn—how much I'd see! Just walking the streets I'd be in the middle of this incredible archaeological site. I mean, the Pantheon. The Forum. The Colosseum." I pause, out of breath. "Dillon, don't."

"Don't what?" he asks.

"Don't be upset about this. I know it means we'll be apart, but only for nine months and it's *Rome*."

"So you want to go?" His gaze flashes up, pain slashing

across his features in the candlelight. "You want to leave me?"

"Of course not," I say. "I'm not leaving you."

"If we're not together, we're apart."

I shake my head. "There might be distance between us, but I love you, Dillon. You know that."

"And you made me swear we'd always be together," he says. "Forever. Remember that night? You said it was a sacred promise."

"It was. It is."

How could I ever forget?

It was October, and Dad and I had been in the new house for about six months by then. I thought he was getting stronger. Steadier. Then the final divorce papers came. By the time I got home, he was sitting in the hallway in a pile of broken glass. Every family picture had been pulled from the wall, smashed on the tile. A stack of legal papers smoked, the edges charred black. I tried to take care of Dad all on my own, but he was beyond drunk. I couldn't get him off the floor.

I called Dillon and he came over. He helped me put Dad to bed. I swept up the glass and sprayed air freshener to clear the smell of smoke. Then I let Dillon hold me, and that night when he said he loved me for the first time, I said I needed it to be forever. I made him promise, as though that would solve everything. But in a way it did. I knew that Dillon was there for me, no matter what.

"This doesn't change any of that," I say. "It's just an internship."

"Do you want it more than you want me?"

His words slap me.

"Dillon. It's not a choice."

"And if it was? Would you give it up?"

"Would you want me to?"

His eyes are black and unreadable. "You're not answering the question."

"I can't believe you're even asking it."

"How would you feel if it was me?" he says. "If I just decided, last-minute, I was going to move next year. See ya later."

My mouth goes dry at the thought. But that's not what I'm saying.

"I made a commitment to you," he adds. "I thought you made the same commitment to me."

"It's an internship." I'm repeating myself, I know I am, but I can't think what else to say. It's like we're playing charades and I keep giving him the same clue because maybe if I say it enough times he'll finally get it. *It's an internship.* "I can't believe we're even having this conversation," I say, trying again. I draw in a long breath and meet his gaze, willing myself to find the words he needs to hear. "It's a great opportunity for me. Yes, it will be horrible to be apart. I will miss you every day and every night. But if I have a shot to go there, to live a year with my feet on two thousand years of history—how can you not want me to go?"

"I want you to have opportunities, Em. Of course I do. But there are all kinds of them right here. You've told me that yourself."

"But they're not Rome." I clench my fists in frustration. "You know classical archaeology is going to be my focus. We've talked about going to Italy a million times."

"Yeah, and we were always going together."

"This is crazy, Dillon. You don't get to decide this."

"And you do?"

"It's my life!"

"I thought it was going to be *our* life!"

I shove back my hair with one hand. "You're twisting everything I say."

"Then say the only thing that matters." His face is set, his eyes burning with emotion.

"Say what?"

"Say that you won't go. Say that you won't leave me."

I want to tear the sheet in my hands. "I'm not leaving you. Not ever. Don't you believe me when I say I love you?" We've never fought like this before, and I can hardly believe it's us. This is the most exciting thing to ever happen to me. He has to see that. *He will. He'll think about it, and he'll see.* I swallow, the taste of my earlier excitement like chalk in my throat.

"You know what?" I say. I'm proud at how calm I sound. How controlled. I sound like Dillon. "We'll talk about this when you get back. We're both tired now and it's been a crazy week. And I need to get home." I whirl around, scooting to the edge of the bed. I reach for my underwear and pull it on. My stomach is a twisted mess, not calm at all. I shake out my jeans with trembling hands and shove a leg in. My toes catch on a frayed hole in the knee and the material rips loudly. It feels like the sound comes from inside of me.

I hear him dressing, too. He's waiting for me to say it's okay, that it doesn't matter. But this isn't just about what kind of music is playing on the car radio.

I can wait, too. I slow my movements, hoping he'll say something while I tug on my sandals, while I reach for my sweater and my purse. This internship means too much. I can outwait him.

Please, Dillon. It feels like my heart beats to his name.

I turn around, wanting him to make this okay. My breath catches. He's sitting on the edge of the bed, his back to me. His jeans are on, but his chest is bare. He's bent over, his fingers pressed to his temples. The slope of his back is strangely vulnerable. Dillon is only eighteen, but he's already so much of a man. So strong and steady. It hurts to see him like this.

"Dillon?" His name whispers out like a wish.

"People leave," he says. He turns enough that I can see the dark line of his square jaw and the shadow of his lowered eyelashes. "And then they never come back."

I sink onto the bed, my anger gone. I suddenly realize what this is really about. His dad. Of course he's thinking about his dad. How he left. How he never came home.

Dillon once told me that he grew up in a house of goodbyes. His dad was a freelance journalist and traveled whenever a job came up. Promises of birthdays and Little League games were forgotten when a war cropped up or a disease broke out. Dillon would wake up and find his father gone, never knowing when he'd be back. Or if.

Three years ago, his dad left to cover a hostage situation in Africa. He died in a helicopter crash in a remote region with a name Dillon can't even pronounce.

"You aren't getting rid of me so easily." I move to his side of the bed, and when I sit beside him, Dillon's warm arms encircle me as he pulls me onto his lap and hugs me tight. My

25

face finds the hollow at the base of his neck and I curl into him, his chin rubbing back and forth over my head.

"We're arguing about something that may never happen," I say. "I have to apply for it along with everyone else. I probably won't get it."

"And if you do?"

"We'll deal with it then." I pull away, just enough that I can look into his beautiful eyes. "Go on the cruise tomorrow, have a great time. Just . . . relax. You need that, Dillon. Eat too much. Swim with the jellyfish."

"Jellyfish have stingers."

"Then swim with the little Nemo fish."

His expression softens into a smile. "Was that the Disney movie you made me watch?"

"And you liked it."

"I like you." His smile fades. "I couldn't live without you, Em. I wouldn't want to."

4

"Enough," Lauren says. She collapses on the bed, bouncing enough to make the coils groan.

I groan, too, as I shove a heavy box full of books and DVDs across the floor until it's next to the other boxes by the door. I straighten and wipe the sweat off my forehead with the back of my arm. My hands are filthy and my blue T-shirt is streaked with dirt. The closet is packed up and the desktop is empty of everything but dust motes that shimmer in the morning light. *Afternoon,* I correct myself. It's a few minutes past two. I roll my shoulders back and feel the ache work all the way down my spine. "We haven't even started your dresser."

"You do the dresser," she says. "I'll nap." Her eyes are closed, her chest rising with a deep breath. I'm still not used to her with short hair. For as long as I can remember she's worn it down to her shoulder blades like mine. It's cute, though—her thick waves are cut so they're fuller on top and wispy where they end near her chin. Still, the new look makes her face seem thinner and older. She's twenty, a college sophomore; it's not as if she's still twelve. I don't know why I still see her that way in my head sometimes. Maybe it's this room.

Exhaustion creeps up on me. After I left Dillon's last night, it took a long time for me to fall asleep, and then I had to be up early to drive fifty-five miles across the city to the house that used to be home. I wasn't thrilled to spend the first morning of spring break boxing up a room, but I'm glad for the distraction. It's kept me from worrying about last night.

"We'll both nap," I say. I shove her shoulder until she scoots over and then I lie beside her on the bed, our elbows touching. The double bed used to seem so big when we were little. A wave of sadness that's been threatening all morning finally washes over me. I'm not sure if I'm sad for the way things used to be or sad about the way things are now.

"It's a good thing," Lauren says. She almost always knows what I'm thinking. She's not only my big sister, but she's always been my closest friend, too. "This house is from a past life, you know? We may be packing up all the stuff today, but it's been empty for a long time."

"It isn't," I say. "It's full of memories."

"The memories we can take with us. The rest of it . . ." She makes a noise in her throat. Something clatters from below and there's a sharp breaking noise followed by Mom's muted curse. A broken plate, maybe. Lauren told her just to donate all of it—Henry already has dishes. But Mom wants to save it. *For you girls,* she said. As if dishes are what we really want her to save.

"This room should be demolished," Lauren says. "It's like

a shrine to my high school self. I look at that poster and I want to shoot myself."

The poster is from the first Twilight movie, and it's tacked to the ceiling above us, carefully taped around the edges to protect it from the ceiling fan. A brooding Taylor Lautner has long hair and an intense stare. "I remember when you hung it up. Even then I thought it was weird. He never seemed like your type—you don't even like dogs."

"But he was so tortured—just look at that expression. I wanted to save him from that bitch Bella." Lauren shudders. "I like to think of it as my one lapse in judgment."

"You're actually admitting to one?" I say with pretend shock.

She gives me a patented Lauren smile—lips pursed with just the barest tilt to the left corner. Dad jokes that they could tell Lauren was going to be a judge from the day they handed her a rattle and she started banging it like a gavel.

Now she's prelaw at U of A, and *Stupidity is not a defense* is her favorite expression. She'll be a great lawyer and an even better judge. She can cut through all the bullshit to the heart of any issue. Lauren's never cared about what-ifs the way I do. Sometimes I think it would be easier if I were more like her.

She sighs. "Everything about this room feels so dated."

"Because it's been two years since you've lived here." I pause. "It's been almost a year for me, and even before that I was spending weekends at Dad's."

The air conditioner kicks on with a hum, and a scarf hanging from the doorknob flutters in the flow of cool air. "Lauren . . . ," I say. The question hovers on my tongue, the way it's hovered deep in my heart since the beginning of my junior year. "If I hadn't seen them hugging that day, if I hadn't said anything, do you think Mom and Dad would still be together?"

"It's not your fault."

"Dad wouldn't have had to move out—the affair could have run its course. Fizzled out, maybe."

"The marriage would have ended anyway. Eventually."

Would it? Or would we all still be together? It's the unanswerable question that keeps me up some nights.

Lauren turns to look at me. "Have you told Dad she's moving in with Henry?"

I can't meet Lauren's eyes.

"Emma, come on," she says. "The house sold over a month ago. He needs to know."

I swallow, miserable. Even Taylor Lautner seems to be staring at me accusingly.

"Fine. I'll tell him." Lauren blows out a breath and I can literally feel the heat of her frustration. "We're meeting for lunch next Sunday. I'll tell him then."

"No!"

"Someone has to, Emma."

"What if he goes over the edge again?"

"You'll be there to take care of him."

"Don't say it like that."

"Like what?"

"Like it's such a bad thing. He's our dad."

"That's the point," she says. "He's your father, not your child. You already gave up your senior year. You shouldn't have to babysit him."

"I didn't *give up* my senior year. I made a few sacrifices."

I roll my eyes—we've been over this so many times before. "I couldn't stay at Centennial anyway—not after discovering that my mother was sleeping with the assistant principal. Kind of puts a damper on things." *Understatement of the century.* "Anyway. It was better to move than watch Mom get a restraining order on Dad."

"But he still thinks she's coming back," Lauren says. "He always has."

When the affair first came out, they tried counseling for a few months, but Mom insisted she needed space. So just after Christmas, Dad rented a house clear across the city. He was sure that Mom would miss him and beg him for forgiveness. But there was no begging. She asked for a divorce in March, and the day after school let out in May, I officially moved in with him. But even with fifty-five miles and a divorce decree between them, he's sure she's coming back.

"He's living in Fantasyland," Lauren says.

"Maybe he's happier that way. Maybe it's what he needs."

She shakes her head. "The truth is always better."

My thoughts shift to Dillon. "But it's not always easier."

"Is he still drinking too much?" she asks.

"Once in a while he'll go on a binge. But usually it's just a glass of wine in the evening. I think it helps him sleep." I shrug. "He misses her."

"Then he's an idiot."

"You're so cynical," I say.

"And you still believe in fairy tales."

"Me? I'm not the one with a werewolf on my ceiling."

She laughs, the same deep belly laugh I have, and the tension that's gathered around us fades.

"Anyway," I say. "I might not be around to take care of him."

Her eyes widen and she turns on her side, resting her cheek on her hand. "Tell me."

I fill her in about the meeting with Mrs. Lyght and the museum internship and the American University of Rome.

"Is it logistically possible?" she asks, and I nod, having known that her first thoughts would be the practical ones.

"I went online last night and checked it out." *It's not like I could sleep.* "The deadline is coming up, so I'd have to request a late decision. But my grades and test scores are high enough, so all I need to do is write a couple of essays and get a recommendation."

"Emmie, that's perfect!"

"It's not a gimme. If I decide to apply, then I'll have to do some sort of assignment, and there's competition, mostly from college kids. I'm supposed to think about it over spring break and then get back to Mrs. Lyght next Monday."

"What's to think about?"

"It's a big change." I lick my lips. "There's also the financial part of it. I researched that last night, too. If I go to ASU, I get a tuition waiver because Dad's a professor there. But if I do the study abroad, I have to pay full program fees. Plus, I have to cover travel and higher living expenses."

"So what. You have a college fund—that's what it's for. Plus, you can apply for financial aid if you need to."

There's a small tear near the hem of my T-shirt. I work my pinky nail through the material, then quickly try to smooth the ragged edges together again. "There's also Dillon."

"Dillon? What does he have to do with this?"

"He's my boyfriend, Lauren. I can't just disappear for a year without considering him."

"Yeah," she says, "you can."

I roll my eyes again, but deep down I love the fierce certainty in her voice. "He's still getting used to the idea," I say. But is he? I have no way of knowing. This morning there was no message on my phone, and by now he's on his way to California and the cruise—without his cell phone. His mom made him promise to leave it at home.

"He better get used to it," Lauren says in her Judge Judy voice, "because you're going."

I tug at the hole in my shirt again. "So you don't think leaving for an internship is total betrayal?"

She gives me a pointed look. "I'm pretty sure we both know what betrayal looks like."

I smile.

"All you're doing is taking advantage of a great opportunity," she adds. "In fact, Dillon should be pushing you out the door. And if he whines about it, tell him he's free to sleep with whomever he wants while you're gone."

I smack her. "You're going to die a lonely old cat lady."

"The only reason I have a cat is because *Dillon* is allergic to fur. Cleo is still your cat."

"She's happier with you."

"Whatever you need to tell yourself to sleep at night." She slants me a serious look. "But you're not giving up anything else for this guy. Especially not an internship in Rome."

"I won't have to."

She quirks an eyebrow in question.

"It's not going to come to that," I say. "We'll talk about it and work through it like the mature adults that we are."

"Ha!" she says. "You mean you think he'll see it your way."

I shift, flipping my ponytail so it's off the pillow. "He will. It just makes sense."

"What if he's thinking the same thing about you?"

"He's not." But her words find their mark, sinking into my suddenly nervous stomach. *I made a commitment to you.* I can hear the hurt in his voice. "Why does everything have to be so complicated?"

"Most things aren't," she says. "It's people who create the complications. If you know what you want, you go out and get it. It's simple."

"And if it hurts others?"

"What's the alternative—to hurt yourself instead? How does that make sense?"

"I wish I could be more like you."

Her face softens into a smile. "I wish you didn't have to be."

"Have to be what?"

Startled, I look toward the door. Mom is leaning against the doorjamb, smiling at us. My whole body stiffens.

"Hey," Lauren says. "We didn't hear you."

"I didn't mean to interrupt," Mom says. She crosses her arms over her chest and then uncrosses them and tucks one hand in a pocket of her too-tight jeans. She's thinner than ever and has started wearing skinny jeans and layered T-shirts. Maybe that's what all the moms with little kids do—now that she's got little kids again. Henry's kids. Personally, I don't think she looks very good. You can see every wrinkle in her neck.

"It's so wonderful to see you both like this," she says. "Brings back so many good memories."

Her words, her cheery voice—they make me sick to my stomach. Most of my memories are from last year, and none of them are good. I turn so my back is to Mom. I don't want to hate her, but I can't help it. I flash Lauren a quick look. "I need to go."

"Emma, don't. Please," Mom says. I can hear her shifting, hear the slight squeak of the door moving. "I got us a pizza. Barbecue chicken and pineapple."

"I'm not hungry."

"Emma. Honey."

Lauren slides to the edge of the bed. "Don't push, Mom."

It's a sign of how screwed up this is when Lauren is the understanding one.

"I'm not pushing," she says. "But how are we going to work through this, Emma, if you won't talk to me?"

I sit on the carpet and pull on my sneakers, tugging them up my ankles rather than untying the knots. "I talk to you."

"One-word texts. Five-minute phone calls."

"Mom," Lauren says.

"If we can just have a conversation," she pleads.

"What are you going to say that you haven't already said?" I shoot to my feet and reach for my purse before facing her. "You slept. With the assistant principal. Of my high school." Tears I can't stop scald my eyes. "That's just . . . gross. What you did to us—to Daddy—is just gross." I swipe at a cheek, horrified that my feelings are so close to the surface, that I still let hurt and anger undo me every single time.

Mom's eyes are wet, too. Her tears make me want to scream. She *chose* to have an affair. She *chose* to leave. And it was her choice to make Henry and his two little boys more important than us.

How do you go to a new life when you have to climb over the wreckage of the old one?

How do you leave your daughter to clean up your mess?

I shoulder my purse. "I've got to go, Lauren. I'll call you later, okay?"

"Okay," she says. She pulls me to her for a quick hug and I'm grateful for that second to get control of myself.

When I reach the door, Mom holds her ground for a long second. "I love you, Emma."

Then she steps aside and I run down the stairs and out of a house that's no longer my home. I'll tell Dad the truth. I'll tell him tonight.

5

Marissa only lives three blocks away and I could get to her house with my eyes closed, so it's not hard to do with tears blurring my vision. I pull into the driveway and take a minute to catch my breath.

I text Marissa:

Just pulling up

I meant to text before I left Mom's, but Marissa knows to expect me. It'll be good to hang out awhile. Marissa always knows the right thing to say, and besides, I can tell her about Rome. Who knows, if it works out, maybe she'll want to come out for a visit.

When the front door opens, Marissa is standing there barefoot, pink bikini straps showing beneath a long tank.

"Hi," I say. "Sorry for the late notice."

"No worries." She smiles but looks a little flushed as she holds open the door.

"Everything okay?"

"I'm trying on bathing suits, which is always a disaster."

I step inside and give her a quick hug. "I meant to get here earlier. I didn't think it would take so long."

"How was it?"

Before I can answer, frenzied barking fills my ears and Charlie, her hyper Australian shepherd, comes flying down the tiled entry, skidding as he barrels into my legs and sends me back into the door.

I laugh and hold out a hand so he can sniff and lick before I move on to rubbing his ears the way he likes. He leaps up, over and over, pawing and sniffing and yipping until Marissa pushes him away. "Quit it, Charlie. She's not here to see you. Go get a treat."

As if he understands all of that and not just "treat," Charlie turns back toward the kitchen, his nails clacking on the tile.

"He misses you," she says.

"I miss him, too." I sigh. I miss *this*. I glance around the familiar entry and down to the sunken living room. "New couch?" I ask, and even that feels familiar.

"You know Mom. Can't pass an estate sale without finding something."

Mrs. Mann peeks around the kitchen. "Emma, I thought I heard your voice. So nice to see you. Everything good?"

"Great."

"Any plans for spring break?"

"No. Just going to hang out with my dad."

"I'll bet he'll love every minute of that. Give him my best, won't you? And before you go, I'll make up a plate of cookies for you to take home." Mrs. Mann has been friends with my mom for years, but she always asks after Dad and I love that about her.

"He'd like that," I say. I sniff and catch the faint scent of chocolate. "Smells good."

"Just put the first batch in."

She disappears back into the kitchen as Marissa heads for the staircase.

"Come on up," she says. "Sarah's here."

I pause with one foot on the first stair. "Sarah?"

"She's helping me pick a suit."

A shadow moves from above and I see Sarah's long blond hair flop over the railing. "Hey, Emma."

"Hey." I like Sarah. I always have. But that doesn't change the fact that today was supposed to be just us and Marissa knew that.

She gives me a look that says, *Sorry.* There's a crease between her brows, a sign that she feels bad. I tell myself to shrug it off. I'm sure it was Sarah, inviting herself over, and Marissa would never hurt anyone's feelings, even under threat of torture. But I'm not in the mood to shrug off anything.

"We need your opinion," Sarah says. "I like this one Marissa's wearing, but she thinks it's too pink."

I follow Marissa up the carpeted steps. "You didn't think it was too pink when you bought it?"

"I bought four to try on," she says over her shoulder. "And I didn't think it was quite *this* pink."

"You bought four and you're trying them on now? Don't you leave tomorrow?"

"You know me," she says.

Sarah laughs as if she knows, too, and of course she does. Everyone in our group of friends knows how much Marissa dreads buying a new bathing suit. She always says her legs are too short for her body so she looks stumpy. But Sarah's laugh still grates on my nerves. Since I moved away, Sarah has been on Marissa like a flea. She's always fluttering around and impossible to get rid of. Marissa and I have talked about it—how it's stupid that I'm jealous and how she feels the same about my new friends. About Dillon. But Dillon is different—he's a boyfriend. Sarah is trying to be me.

Marissa rolls her eyes as she tugs her shirt down over her legs. "If only the fashion was to have overendowed thighs, I'd be a supermodel."

"Stop it," Sarah says. "I think you look great. You have to try on the green one for Emma, too."

Marissa's room is dotted with stacks of shorts, T-shirts, and a pile of swimwear, some of it still on hangers on top of her desk. Sitting on the carpet, half packed, are duffels.

Two of them.

I look from the duffels to Marissa.

"Sarah's coming with," she says.

"To Mexico? With your family?"

Sarah moves a stack of T-shirts and sits on the bed. "My mom would never let me go to Rocky Point, but she says it's okay if I go with responsible adults." She smiles wryly. "She wanted to give Marissa's parents a polygraph, but I got her to back down."

I'm still watching Marissa, wondering why she didn't tell

me. We just talked . . . well, we exchanged texts a few days ago. Definitely less than a week. "You didn't say."

"It was one of those last-minute things."

Like Sarah being here today? The words are on the tip of my tongue. I'm suddenly close to tears. This day has been too much already. "You know what? I thought this was a good time, but you guys are busy."

"Emma."

"No, it's okay. I'm really beat anyway. But have a great trip."

"Wait, don't," Marissa says. She reaches the door before me and grabs the knob. "Don't leave mad."

"I'm not mad," I say. "It's just been a hard day." I lower my voice. "I thought it was just going to be us."

"You weren't even sure if you were going to make it over."

"I wasn't sure what time."

"That's what you always say," Sarah interjects, as though she's a part of this conversation.

I whirl to face her. "What?"

She's still sitting on the bed, her hands bearing her weight, her shoulders raised in an easy shrug, but I read the challenge in her overly mascaraed eyes. "You say that you're not sure what time or that you'll be late or that you have to leave early, and most of the time you don't show at all."

"That was one time."

"What about her birthday?"

"Sarah!" Marissa says, her cheeks flushing.

I feel flushed, too, hot with anger and resentment. "I came over. I took her to lunch."

41

"On Saturday. But you said you'd show up on Thursday."

"It was a school night. I had homework." I look at Marissa. "I told you. You knew that." I pause, waiting for her to back me up. "Marissa?"

Her arms are hugging her chest, shoulders hunched, her eyes down like she wishes she were anywhere else. "We're all busy. I understood."

"Please," Sarah says under her breath so that I can barely hear it. But I do hear it and I know there's more I should say but there's also a lump in my throat and a heaviness behind my eyes. I don't want to lose it, not in front of Sarah.

"When do you get home from Mexico?" I ask Marissa.

"Saturday," she says.

"I'll call you. Saturday night. We'll set up something for the week after. Okay?"

"Perfect," she says.

I pull her to me and give her a hug. Over her shoulder I glare at Sarah, who's watching me like I'm in the wrong. Does she think she's protecting Marissa? From me?

I step back and open the bedroom door. "Have a great time," I say. Then I pin Marissa with a firm look. "Saturday," I say again.

The house is quiet when I get home. I set my purse on the counter with my keys. "Dad?"

It's just after six and though it's been a long day, the sun is still bright through the window that stretches above the kitchen table.

I decorated when I moved in, hanging blue ready-made

curtains over the windows and buying bright yellow cushions for the chairs along with matching place mats. I laid a fluffy blue rug by the sink and dangled striped blue-and-yellow pot holders from hooks beside the cooktop. I'm not sure what I was hoping to accomplish—as if Dad would see the pot holders and think, *Gee, those make me so happy, I'll stop missing Mom.* I guess I hoped that if I could somehow make it *look* like a home, then it would actually be one.

I'm tired. Maybe it's good that the house is sold. I've only been back a few times, for holidays or when Lauren is home for a visit, but every time I'm there it makes me feel worse. It's not just Mom. It's everything, even Marissa.

I'm still mad about the things Sarah said. She's wrong— she is—but I have to admit that it's been hard to connect with Marissa. There's always so much going on, and it's not like she lives around the corner anymore. I hate that I felt the distance when I hugged her goodbye. I'll fix it, though. Just as soon as she gets back.

I let my eyes drift shut. I want Dillon to be here so badly—I want to lean into him instead of this cold kitchen counter. "Hold me," I'd say, and he'd put down whatever he's doing and pull me against his chest and we'd stay like that, my head on his shoulder, his hands warm at the small of my back. After a few minutes, he'd say, "Come sit," and I'd end up on the couch with my feet in his lap and his hands doing magical things as he massaged. "My turn next," I would promise, and he would nod, and then we'd both smile because I'm terrible at massages and it's never his turn and he never cares. God, I miss him so much.

The fight we had is still in the back of my mind like a bug

bite you forget you have until suddenly it starts to itch. I want to imagine us making up, but it's the one thing I can't picture. We almost never fight.

A drawer clangs shut in the small office off the master bedroom. My eyes flash open. "Dad?" I call again.

"Back here, baby."

I straighten and gather myself in a steadying breath. I need to do this now. I'll tell him about the move and then I'll tell him I need him to keep it together. I need him to be a responsible dad—just for a little while longer.

But when I get to the door of his office, I freeze. I want to sink to the carpet. No. That's not true. I want to turn away and let someone else deal with this. But there is no one else.

The room is a wreck. The desk and chair are covered with old photos and the credenza is piled with things I recognize from a tub of scrapbooking supplies I collected when I went through a phase a few years ago. The family photo albums are lying open on the rug beneath his desk. Dad is sitting in the middle of the albums, a bottle of wine lying empty on its side. A second one is barely balanced on the edge of his desk. Perfect. He's picked today to fall apart.

There's a glass in his hands, the wine sloshing like purple waves as he takes a drink and looks up at me with a sweet smile. "How was your day? How were all my favorite girls?"

I can almost hear Lauren's voice in my head: *Tell him now—how much worse can it get?*

"Dad," I say, "let's get you off the floor."

He shakes his head. "I'm making a memory book. For your mom."

"Oh." I inject just enough enthusiasm in my voice so he's

relaxed and unsuspecting as I pull the glass out of his hand and set it on the desk. I glance around the room again.

What would an archaeologist think if they uncovered this space a thousand years from now? They'd find pictures of smiling parents. Two little girls in matching pajamas growing up in a series of Christmas photos that abruptly ended when Lauren turned eleven and balked at the humiliation. There are homemade birthday cards hanging from a small corkboard and a little statuette with wide arms that says I LOVE YOU THIS MUCH. Would a historian conclude that a happy family had lived here? Or would they dig deeper and notice that as the smiling parents got older, the space between their faces got wider and wider? First the faces of children appeared between them, and then just . . . space. Would they look at the wreckage in this room and see a search for something missing? Or would they see what it actually was—a search for what had been lost?

I think of Dillon and my throat tightens. We will never get to this place. Never.

I move the wine bottle and uncover a stack of clippings Dad must have pulled out of a box from the attic. I shuffle through them as if they're snapshots from the years of their marriage. Dad's smiling face behind a desk as trips are announced to Egypt and Macedonia and Turkey. Always that same photo as if time touched everything except the historian.

"Silly, wasn't it?" He looks up at me, and my heart hurts from the pain in his swollen eyes.

"What, Dad?"

"I used that same awful photo for fifteen years."

"You didn't have time to sit still for another one."

"I never had time for too many things." He rubs a hand over his face and looks around. He's wearing plaid pajama bottoms and a rumpled ASU T-shirt that's so old and faded only the *S* is still readable. But it's like everything else from our past life. He can't let it go.

He has nice eyes, clear blue when he isn't drinking, and even with the new lines etched into his face over the past year he seems scholarly rather than old. His hair is more salt than pepper, but he still has plenty of it. He's a handsome guy. He looks like one of those dads on TV you wish were your own.

Which is who he used to be.

"I was watching a movie this afternoon. Something embarrassingly sentimental." He scratches at the back of his neck. "The man put together an album of photos and left it for the woman. It seemed like a good idea." He smiles and shrugs. "Memories of the two of us to remind her of what we had. But then I couldn't find any pictures of just the two of us. There were vacations and school events and Lauren's moot court competitions. Sometimes the four of us, but usually the three of you, and when I was there, I was behind the camera. Observing. The role of the historian." His voice is sad. "Not so good an observer after all."

"Dad."

His head hangs. "We only see once it's too late." He closes an album, a tiny tremor running across his rigid shoulders. Shaking free of ghosts—that's what it reminds me of when he does that. "How is she?" he asks.

"Fine. She's fine."

46

"Did you two talk things out?"

"There's nothing for us to talk about."

"Emma, you can't keep shutting her out. It doesn't help anything. It could be part of what's keeping us all separated."

I stare at him in disbelief. "It's not what's keeping us separated."

Dad's throat works up and down. "He wasn't there, was he?"

"No."

His shoulders dip with relief. The shadow of a smile lifts the corners of his mouth. "Mom and I have exchanged some emails about Lauren. About arranging an apartment for her this summer and the tone has been so friendly. She's all alone in that big house and I think she's starting to feel it, baby."

"Dad." I swallow.

"I'm going to finish this memory book for her birthday in three weeks. She'll like it, don't you think?"

"Dad," I say again. Gently. Firmly. "There's something I need to tell you."

He brings a hand to his chest and his face lights up. I have to look away. His hope is such a painful, painful thing. A thin, fragile, impossible thing and yet he holds on to it with a death grip. How do I take that away from him?

"Well?" he asks.

"It's about next year." I smile. "How would you feel about me going to Rome?"

I'm being pulled up from under dark blue water . . . tugged to the surface by the sound of a heart beating in rhythm with the waves.

Hmmmm Hmmmm Hmmmm Hmmmm.

I wake suddenly, blinking my eyes open to pitch black and the sound of my phone vibrating. Heart in my throat, I reach for my cell, knocking over a bottle of hand lotion before my fingers find the phone. I slide my finger across the call button. "Hello?"

"Emma!"

"Dillon?" I push myself up, my breath coming hard and fast. "It's the middle of the night. Are you okay?"

"I couldn't sleep." He sounds far away and there's a hum in the background as if a fly is caught on the line. But it's him. It's Dillon.

"Are you still on the cruise?"

"Two more nights."

"But how are you—I didn't think there was a phone."

"I'm not supposed to be calling. It costs almost as much as the cruise."

"Dillon—"

"I don't care," he interrupts. His voice is strained, as if someone has a fist around his lungs. "I had to hear your voice. I hate that we fought."

I sink back and it feels like the only thing holding me up this past week has been worry. Suddenly it's gone and I'm as heavy and limp as a wet towel. I cradle the phone wishing I were touching him instead. "I hate it, too."

"We'll work it out, Em. Our lives are connected—the Red String, remember?"

"Of course I remember." I smile and my eyes feel a tiny bit wet at the corners. "The day you saved my life."

"I'll always save you," he says. "I'll always keep you safe." His breath is ragged over the phone. "I have to go," he says. "My mother will go ballistic when she sees the charges."

I press my cheek harder into the phone. "I'm glad you called. I was worried. I—"

"We'll be together soon." His voice catches, breaks. "For always."

"Dillon?"

There's a sharp click.

"Dillon?"

The phone screen goes dark. I stare at it a second, then press the phone to my chest. My pulse is racing. His voice sounded so strange at the end. It must have been the connection.

Anna is stirring the fish stew when Marcus arrives at her lunch counter. She meets his piercing gray eyes, hopeful. He drops his head, his curls not quite hiding the flush. She fights her disappointment as she reaches for a bowl and a ladle to serve him.

It won't be today.

"My father . . . It must be done carefully," he murmurs.

It is what he says every day. She forces a nod and reminds herself that Marcus Ceillus is from one of the finest families in all of Pompeii. She is lucky to have his love at all.

As if he reads her thoughts, he leans in. "It will not be forever." Then he presses coins for the stew into her palm, along with something else. Something round yet pointed. Her pulse beats furiously as she shifts, turning away from the danger of snooping eyes. When Anna uncurls her fingers, it is all she can do not to cry out.

Lying in her palm is the most beautiful ring she has ever seen. It is a coiled serpent, glimmering in pure gold with a raised head and eyes formed by two dark jewels.

51

"To remind you," Marcus murmurs, "that just as the snake does, we may shed our skin and become reborn."

Anna shakes her head. "I cannot wear this!"

"Keep it for now. As a promise of our future together."

Anna slides the ring deep into the pouch that hangs from the belt of her simple tunic. She is both scared and thrilled. It is the most valuable thing she has ever owned.

A boom suddenly cracks through the sky, making the earth rock with violent shudders. Behind her, shelves of pottery crash and shatter. She and Marcus both grab the counter as screams wail throughout the market.

"It is Jupiter!" someone shouts. "His fury will destroy us all!"

In the sky above the green slope of the mountain, a cloud of black shoots into the heavens. Anna is struck mute as it rises like the angry breath of all the gods and then balloons out in the shape of an enormous tree.

"Run!" cries Treyvus, who works beside her. "I have said this place is cursed!"

And he has—all summer when fish turned up dead in the lakes. When the olives died on the branches and the crops withered in the fields.

The stone road is already choked with merchants and customers, slaves and patricians alike, each rushing toward the gates.

Anna hesitates, looking to Treyvus and then to Marcus.

"We will be safe in my father's villa," he says.

Anna's heart pounds as Treyvus shakes his head, his dark eyes a warning.

Marcus holds out a hand and she only hesitates a second

as her fingers squeeze the hidden ring. Then she slips her hand into his.

"Be safe!" Treyvus shouts one last time as he disappears into the crowd.

Anna's breath shudders like the ground. Shattered pottery surrounds her. The marble counter has cracked and the ground is writhing beneath her feet. Marcus will keep her safe.

There's a Chinese legend called the Red String of Fate. Dad told me about it one Sunday when Mom was showing houses and Lauren and I had to go with him to his office at ASU. Lauren hated going there. She said his whole building smelled like a bologna sandwich. Lauren didn't see the point of collecting old stuff when they were making newer things so much better.

Dad would give her his iPad loaded with a movie and a dollar for the vending machine, and I'd settle down in front of his bookcases and search for anything new. He taught archaeological studies and supervised field expeditions—most of them in the Southwest, which was his area of expertise. But Dad's students would travel to sites all over the world and they always gave him things, thank-you gifts and tokens from the places they'd visited. I could travel around the world and never leave his office.

One day, I discovered a beautiful box carved out of wood

with symbols across the lid that I didn't understand. I held my breath as I opened it, imagining I'd find a bright red ruby or maybe an ancient white opal.

Instead, I looked up at Dad, disappointed. "It's empty!"

"No," he said. "There's something there. Something that can't be seen, only felt." As a shiver ran down my spine, he told me the legend of the Red String of Fate.

In ancient times, it was said that the gods would tie a red string around the ankles of two people who were meant to meet. The two people, connected by the red thread, were destined to be lovers, to find each other no matter the time, place, or circumstances. The red string could be twisted or knotted but never broken so that the two people, upon meeting, would feel the connection.

That's the best way to describe what it was like when I met Dillon. That first time on the trails even before I could see into his eyes. I felt something. A tug. Like a slack fishing line that's suddenly jerked taut with its catch.

It was a year ago in February and icy cold, the way it can get on clear, cloudless days. I was spending the weekend with Dad in a rental house full of someone else's furniture and a refrigerator full of Styrofoam takeout containers. A shoelace broke on my trail runners and I actually cried over it—that was how great I was feeling about everything that Saturday morning.

I had found a system of running trails next to the neighborhood park and was two miles in, wondering where the dirt path led, when I heard them behind me. Pounding feet. Breathless laughter. They were coming up on me fast—too fast. I veered off the trail and under the branches of a spindly tree as two guys came sprinting around the corner. A taller, lankier guy was in back, but that was about all I noticed of him. My eyes were drawn to the boy in front, dark hair ruffling in the wind created by his own speed. He'd pulled away by at least four strides, but he still threw his arms back and his chest forward as if a finish line stretched across the trail. And he was smiling. Laughing really. There was such freedom in that smile. So much *joy*. My chest felt warm, my own heart pounding in response—to what I wasn't sure.

Just past the tree they slowed to a stop, dust kicking up around them. They both bent over, their backs to me, drinking air. "You crowded me out," the tall one said.

"I wanted to but you were too far behind."

There was shoving and more laughing.

"Let's go again."

"I'm ready." They straightened, turned, and that was when they saw me.

"Oh. Hey," the tall one said. He had friendly eyes and dimples that suggested he was the kind of guy who smiled a lot. "Didn't see you there."

"I was trying to stay out of the way."

"Did we run you off the trail?" I looked at his friend, his eyes hidden by reflective sunglasses, his smile nothing but polite. Still, my heart raced. In my head, I could see him crossing the imaginary finish line. I wondered what it would be like to have him smile at me like that.

"No, that's okay," I said. "I was going to turn around anyway. I wasn't sure how far the loop runs."

"Four miles around if you don't veer off," the tall one said. "If you like hills, we can show you a great turnoff up ahead."

"Oh." I flushed. "That's okay."

His friend gave him a look. "She's not going to go off with us on a trail. She doesn't know who we are."

"We're nice guys. I'm Jace. This is Dillon." He paused, his eyebrows raised.

"Emma," I finally said.

"Nice to meet you, Emma. We're very trustworthy. Scout's honor." He held up four fingers.

I tried not to laugh. "I think that's the Vulcan thing from *Star Trek*."

He looked at his fingers as if he were disappointed in them. "Oh, right."

"But we are trustworthy," Dillon said. "Don't let his shoes scare you."

"What's wrong with my shoes?" Jace asked.

"I wouldn't trust a guy wearing shoes like that."

I studied the neon green runners and another laugh bubbled up. "They are a little bright," I said.

"A little?" Dillon repeated.

"They'd look good with a crossing guard vest."

Dillon grinned and I grinned back.

"You live around here?" he asked.

I shook my head. "My dad's living in the neighborhood for a while, so I've been coming here on the weekends."

"Well"—he ruffled his hair—"if you're looking for a good cup of coffee, there's a place called Cupz just across from the high school."

"Thanks," I said.

"Maybe we'll see you there," Jace added.

I smiled. "Maybe so." It was Jace I answered but Dillon I couldn't take my eyes off.

I found myself thinking about him all week—about his smile as he sprinted past, about what his eyes might look like behind those sunglasses. Even when I scolded myself for being ridiculous, something drew my mind back to the trails, back to him.

I didn't know it yet, but it was the Red String.

The next two days of spring break feel more like two weeks. I've filled my time by going through the application for the university in Rome. Dad insisted on paying the initial fee—*Think positive!*—and I submitted the online registration form. I have to write a personal statement and I've already started on my essay about "What *All Roads Lead to Rome* Means to Me."

Then Hannah got back today and texted to see if I wanted to meet for a coffee. We don't usually hang out, just the two of us, so I'm especially glad she suggested it. We've arranged to meet here, at Cupz. I'm early, but it's nice to get out of the house.

I sip a vanilla cappuccino as I settle deeper into one of the leather chairs. The table beside me is sticky with something that looks like grape jelly. I don't even care; I'm just glad not to be at home. Dad has also been off this week for ASU's spring break, and I need to be where he isn't. The album has kept him busy, but it's hard to watch him working on it as if it'll change everything. The one good thing is that he's been helping me brush up on my knowledge of Rome. He pulled together a pile of books on the city, including some articles from his professional journals. But I don't want to get my hopes up—I haven't even seen the assignment yet.

Still. I keep wondering what Rome will really be like—all the things pictures can't tell you. When I run, will the dirt be light tan and dry like it is here, or will it be a damp reddish brown? Will the air smell like baking bread? Is the Pantheon really that big inside? There are so many questions swirling around in my head, and Dillon is the question mark hovering over them all. I want to share this with him. Will we be able to talk about it when he's back tomorrow? I'm so anxious to see him, especially since his call on Thursday. I knew we'd be okay—how could we not? I look over at the condiments counter, the stacks of napkins and straws, the tubs of sugar and artificial sweeteners, and I can see back to the first time we stood there, talking.

I met Dillon on the trails, but Cupz is where we got to know each other.

I didn't go that first Saturday, but when I stopped in the following weekend, they were both there—Jace and Dillon. I discovered that Jace had his own reusable coffee mug because he was worried about landfills and that they both played baseball for Ridgeway High. And that Dillon's eyes were a deep sapphire blue. I saw them again the following week and the week after that.

Then one Saturday in March, Jace was sick and it was just Dillon and me. It was only a few days after the police had found Dad passed out on Henry's lawn. We were standing at the condiments counter and Dillon asked how things were and I started to cry. He paled, immediately saying he was sorry, and I said no, I was sorry, and some guy behind us asked if we could be sorry somewhere else because he needed creamer before his coffee got cold.

Dillon and I sat at a table—the one by the front window that gets too much sun, but it felt just right that morning. I told him my mom had asked my dad for a divorce and that my dad wasn't moving home, and they weren't going to work things out. "It's for the best," I said, because that was what I'd been saying to Marissa and Lauren and to my dad when he was sober enough to hear me.

"You really think that?" Dillon asked.

I completely broke down then because of course I didn't. My usual polite responses, the ones meant to make other people feel okay, dried up. Dillon told me about his dad dying and how he was always looking for silver linings that didn't exist. It felt like finally someone understood.

I told him I couldn't stay with my mom and that I was going to move in with my dad when school ended. He leaned in and his fingers curved around his cup. "Maybe there is a silver lining after all," he said.

And when I smiled, he looked at me like it mattered—my smile. Like my happiness mattered.

That Saturday turned into more Saturdays through the end of March, April, and then May. Some mornings I'd see them on the trails first and sometimes I'd find Dillon and Jace already at Cupz arguing over designated hitters or whether hens really cared about laying eggs in cages or not. I got acquainted with Jace's bizarre collection of running shoes and I met Hannah and Spence and Lydia. Weekends spent taking care of my dad became weekends when I might see Dillon. But I was never sure if he liked me or if he was just being nice. Because he was. Nice. Until everything changed that day at the community center.

The bell dings over the glass door as it opens. Automatically, I look up at the sound. I wave when I see Hannah.

"Hey!" She walks over in flip-flops and a red T-shirt dress.

"You look great!" And she does. Her tan makes her hair seem blonder and her teeth sparkle like she's just had them whitened. "Cute dress," I say.

"Thanks." She does a quick shimmy that sends the skirt fluttering as she sets down her purse. She fishes out her wallet. "Hang on, I'll get a drink."

A few minutes later she settles beside me with a large iced tea. "Oh Lord, it's good to be back in civilization." She sighs dramatically and I can't help laughing.

"You didn't have a great time?"

She rolls her eyes. "My dad had this brilliant idea of renting a beach bungalow. Apparently *bungalow* is code for portable toilets with blue water and kitchen cabinets with roaches."

"Eww," I say.

"Exactly." She takes a long drink of her tea. "But the beach was nice."

"And your tan is gorgeous."

"Thank you. I'm sure Spence will be unable to resist my

beauty—if he ever sees it." She shoots me an irritated look. "He's going bowling tonight with Ty and Derrick and a few of the other guys."

"Well, good," I say, "then we can hang out. Maybe go to a movie?"

She stirs the ice with her straw. "Missing Dillon, huh?"

"Completely." I smile. "He'll be back tomorrow afternoon."

"Just be ready," she says. "He'll be tired when he gets home. He never sleeps good on vacations."

I force a slight nod as I lower my eyes so she can't see my annoyance. This is what makes me crazy about Hannah. She always has to tell me things about Dillon as if she's the expert. As if she knows him better than I ever will. Dillon says I'm overanalyzing. Maybe, but it doesn't feel like I am.

"So will you see Spence tomorrow?" I ask.

"Only if he begs for forgiveness." She stabs the straw through the ice. "Bowling? Really? On Saturday night? And I just got home."

"Maybe he'd already made plans?"

"Or maybe we've been friends for so long, he forgets I'm his girlfriend now."

"He's comfortable with you—enough to be himself. In a way that's a compliment."

She fake laughs. "Nice try, Emma."

I settle back into the chair with a shrug. "Okay, then he's a complete ass."

"Yes," she says, pointing a finger at me as if I'm on a game show and just came up with the correct answer. Then she tilts her head in thought. "But it is a very nice ass. Does that make me shallow?"

"Women are biologically predisposed to asses."

"Oh, good," she says. "That's a relief." She sets down her tea. "So what movie should we see?"

"You want to?" I pull out my phone. "I'll check the listings."

"Just nothing with Channing. Or either of the Hemsworths."

I slant her a look. "Um. Okay?"

"They'll be gorgeous and sweet and sensitive and I'll be pissed at Spence all over again. I hope you know how lucky you are with Dillon."

"I know."

"Bowling," she mutters under her breath. "What happened to romance? Is it so wrong to want to be wooed?"

"Of course not," I say. "And personally I think you're very wooable." I sweep a hand over my heart and raise the other hand to the sky, as if I'm Romeo standing beneath Juliet's window. "O dearest Hannah, your beauty and graceful form doth stir passion in my manly breast."

She groans. "Forget it. I've changed my mind about wooing."

We're both grinning as I check my phone for a movie. Hannah is right about one thing. I am lucky to have Dillon, and tomorrow I'm going to make sure he knows it. I refocus on the listings. But I already feel like I have my happy ending.

9

I open the door on Sunday afternoon before he's even had time to knock. It feels as if my chest is vibrating with the pounding of my heart. "Hi," I say, breathless. "I heard the truck."

Dillon is standing on the welcome mat, the Sunday-afternoon sun painting a prism in his inky hair. I'm almost dizzy for a second. I've missed him this whole week, but it hits me harder somehow, now that he's here. He holds out his arms, and with a sob of relief I'm pressing myself into his chest, twining my arms around his solid middle. Dillon is like the Palo Verde tree in the back of our old house. Even when monsoon winds whip through the valley strong enough to bring down fences and tear out other trees from the roots, the Palo Verde never bends. Dillon is like that. Steady. Grounded.

Now he smells like sweat and sun and he groans as he wraps his arms tightly around my back.

"Sorry," he says. "I should've showered after seven hours in the car, but I needed to see you. I dropped off my mom and came right over."

His head tilts and I feel him rub his cheek over the top of my hair the way he likes to do, pulling me so close I can hardly breathe. Dillon has a thing about being clean. He showers every morning and every night, even if he just showered after baseball practice. I tease him that that's why his skin is so smooth. He's part seal. "It's okay," I say. "We'll shower together."

He pulls back, his eyes widening. His lashes are short and spiky, as black and fine as his hair. "Where's your dad?"

"He drove to Tucson to have lunch with Lauren." I can picture them at the Blue Willow restaurant, sitting on the back patio right now. I just don't know what they're talking about. Lauren promised not to tell him about Mom moving in with Henry—I hope she keeps her word. But I don't want to think about that now.

"That might be the best news I've ever heard," Dillon says.

He backs me inside, his lips already on mine. We have a lot to talk about, but it can all wait. There's urgency in his mouth, in the weight of his hands as his warm fingers raise my shirt and skim my waist. I feel it, too—an urgency to reconnect. To be close again before words can slip in between us.

I break away long enough to close the door and turn the lock. Then I shriek when Dillon lifts me. He isn't tall—five nine to my five five—but he's built like a wrestler rather than a baseball player. Or maybe it's all the hours crouched behind the plate that's made his thighs as strong as Roman columns.

He carries me now as if I weigh nothing, laughing at my reaction as I grab on to his neck. The sound of his laugh is quite possibly the best thing I've ever heard.

I was right, what I said to Lauren—he has come to see it my way.

Our house is a split plan with Dad's bedroom at one end and my room and bath at the other. The third bedroom is Lauren's, though she's never really used it. Dillon carries me past my room and into the bathroom. He sets me down and locks the door. It's a big room, decorated in white wicker with two sinks, a mirror framed in blue, and white globe lights above. The shower is at the far end, enclosed by sliding glass doors with white and blue tiles from floor to ceiling. I turn on the shower and then face him.

His eyelids are already heavy, his lips parted. "You're wearing too many clothes," he says.

My stomach feels hollowed out. "You've been surrounded by girls in bikinis."

"I never noticed."

"Liar."

He pulls his shirt over his head and sets it on the counter. His shoulders are wide, muscles flexing across his hairless chest and down the contours of his abs. His skin is deeply tanned from the cruise and I can feel warmth coming off him as if he's radiating sunlight.

My throat is dry, my breath shallow as my pulse jumps. "The girls noticed you," I say.

He ignores that, his eyes on my chest. "Your turn."

I lift my tank. I'm wearing a new lacy push-up bra in

Dillon's favorite color, blue. I bought it yesterday with this moment in mind.

His breath hisses out with a groan. "Oh hell."

I smile. The bra is worth every penny I spent. He slides off his shorts and boxers as I slip off my shorts and then, more slowly, my underwear. A blush prickles over my chest and neck. I don't know why I suddenly feel shy, though this is still pretty new for us. We've been together for nearly a year, but we only made love for the first time two months ago. I didn't want to rush into it. Part of it was wanting to be responsible—seeing a doctor and getting started on birth control. But the other part was wanting it to be *right*. Dillon wasn't a virgin, but I was, and it mattered to me, even if I couldn't say exactly why. History, I suppose. Not past history, as in the idea that my virtue as a human being was somehow wrapped up in my virginity—not everything from the past deserved to live on. It was more about *my* history— the moments I would carry around with me always. You don't usually know what things you'll remember forever, but having sex for the first time? I figure that one was pretty much a guarantee. I wanted to be sure it was a memory that would make me smile—not cringe.

And it was.

"Don't," he says.

I blink. "What?"

He slides one finger beneath a bra strap and pulls me close. "Don't be shy with me."

"I don't mean to be."

"It's because we were apart." His gaze is full of love, but

there's also a hint of pain in the tired puffiness beneath his eyes. *It's the fight we had. It's the time away.* Then his mouth closes over mine. He kisses me, bending me backward over his arm. His hand circles my waist and his fingers tighten over my hip bone.

He pulls back, breathing heavy. "I missed you so much," he says. "Too much." His fingers press hard and I exhale from the sting of pain, but he doesn't seem to hear. His eyes are all pupil, as if something dark inside has come to the surface and swallowed him whole—as if it's ready to swallow me.

"Now," he says. "Come with me now." He tugs at me, and my body responds. Heat rises inside me like the steam that fills the room and fogs the mirror. We're a blur of skin, dark and pale, one ending where the other begins. I forget everything but him as he pulls me into the shower.

10

We're lying under the sheets, the pillows damp from our wet hair. The cream duvet is pushed to the floor. The bed is a queen—a present from Dad when I moved in with him. Though we have room to sprawl out, Dillon always takes the middle so we touch, even when it's too hot to want anything against my skin. Now we're both lying on our backs, our fingers entwined on top of the sheet.

"It's good to be home," he says. "It's good to be here."

I smile and squeeze his fingers. Afternoon light filters through my blinds, turning the buttery yellow paint to a rich gold. My gaze skims over the shelves of treasures on the opposite wall. The blue and green mosaic glass plate. The Egyptian pottery jug in deep red with an angled handle that took me hours to piece together. They're both models I reconstructed in junior archaeology camps but the shards of pottery on the bottom shelf all came from actual dig sites. And there's the engraved trowel from Marissa and Dad's old *I Dig*

It! camouflage hat that I wore to every summer dig until it started to fall apart. I smile and squeeze Dillon's hand again. All my favorite treasures are in this room, including him. "I'm glad you're here, too."

"We're never getting a bigger bed," he says. "We're not going to be one of those couples who end up at opposite sides. Not even when we're eighty years old and you snore."

"*I* snore? By then you'll be too deaf to hear if I do."

I can feel his smile. "I should get us one of those cruise ship beds. That'll keep us close."

"How was the cruise?" I tilt my head to look at him but he's staring at the ceiling.

"Long."

"Come on. You must have had a good time. You love the beach." I let go of his hand and shift to my side. I trail a hand over his pecs. I would come back from a cruise five pounds heavier but Dillon looks leaner if anything.

"I love my mom," he says.

"Buuuuut?"

"But she's always *there*. You know? It feels like I'm always onstage, trying to give her the reaction she wants."

"What does she want?"

He sighs, his chest rising beneath my hand. "To know that I'm happy. To know that I'm not going anywhere." He turns to face me. "We had a talk about you."

"Oh, no." I prop myself on one elbow.

"Don't say it like that."

"She doesn't like me."

"She doesn't like the idea of you. At least, she didn't. Before."

I brush away a clump of wet hair that's stuck to my cheek. "That must have been some talk."

He smiles, but it fades almost immediately. "I told you about Kiersten."

I nod. Kiersten was Dillon's one serious girlfriend before me. She went to a private school in Phoenix, but they met at the community center where he lifeguards during the summer. They had one of those intense summer romances, and when it broke up in September, he took it hard. He never said why it ended, just that it didn't work out. I didn't ask for details. I'd had a dozen passionate crushes (mostly unrequited), but I'd never had a serious boyfriend. I didn't want to think of him that close to someone else.

"The breakup was hard on me, and you know my mom. She's overprotective."

"I know."

"Thing is . . . I went through a tough time when my dad died."

"You were fifteen, Dillon. Of course you did."

He wets his lips. "I started having nightmares. I'd dream that my dad was at the door. And when I answered . . ." His breath shudders through him; I'm not sure I want to hear this. I find his hand again and lace my fingers through his. "He's standing there in one of his white button-downs, his hair combed back and still a little wet as if he's going somewhere special. And he's smiling. Just . . . smiling. And under his foot is a bomb." His eyes squeeze shut. "Sometimes it's not a bomb. Sometimes he's holding a grenade. And the pin is pulled. And then—"

"Oh, Dillon," I breathe.

"My mom sent me to a therapist." He opens his eyes to look at me. "Did I ever tell you that?"

I shake my head.

"Just the one time. Anyway, it turns out I struggle with the idea of losing people." He forces a half-smile and I want to crawl inside him and never let go. "So I let the thing with Kiersten get to me more than it should have. My mom worries that you'll turn out to be another Kiersten. That you're going to break my heart. I told her you're not like that." His gaze locks on mine. "I trust you, and so can she."

"Wow." I let that sink in.

"And I want your dad to know the same thing," he adds in a low voice. "That he can trust me."

"It isn't that he doesn't trust you, Dillon, because he does. He worries that we're too young to be so serious."

"But your mom is okay with it?"

"My mom has lost the right to vote on anything related to relationships."

He sighs. "So how was it? Going over there, I mean."

"Hard," I say.

"You sad about the house?"

"More than I expected," I admit.

He raises my hand and tickles my palm with a kiss. "I knew you would be." He kisses the round knob of my wrist bone. "I'm sorry I wasn't here."

"I know."

His lips press against the inside of my forearm. "I hate to think of you hurting."

"It was okay. I had Lauren there."

"And you saw Marissa?"

Marissa! I shoot straight up and nearly knock him in the jaw. "I forgot to call her." I lean over for my phone. "I promised I'd call yesterday."

"She'll understand."

I shake my head. "I promised."

He tugs at the arm he's still holding and plants a kiss on my shoulder. "Can't you wait and call her when I'm gone? What's one more hour going to matter? We've hardly even talked."

I meet the intense blue of his eyes and my fingers go slack on the phone. "Don't let me forget, all right?" I set the phone down and reach for a bottle of water. "What a mess of a week."

"What else happened?"

I hand him the water as he sits up. "I was supposed to tell Dad that the house is sold and Mom is moving in with Henry. But I still haven't, and now Lauren is mad at me."

"Why doesn't she tell him?"

"She wants to, but you should see him, Dillon. He's making a birthday present for my mom and he's just so *happy*. I don't want him to go off the deep end."

He takes a drink and gives me the bottle. "What happens if you go away next year?"

The plastic crackles under my suddenly tight grip.

"It's okay, Em." He takes the bottle from my nervous fingers and sets it on the bedside table. "We need to talk about it, right?"

"We do," I say. I glance at the clock. We have at least another hour before my dad will be home.

"You still want to apply?" he asks.

I hold the sheet tighter to my chest. "Yeah, I do. But that doesn't mean I want to leave you."

"I get that."

I shift to meet his gaze. "You do? Really?"

His lips curve in a smile. "Really."

My breath whooshes out. "I was so afraid you wouldn't understand."

He shakes his head. "If we're going to be together—I mean really together—we have to think about each other. Right?"

"Right."

"And I've had time to think, Em. I can see why you're so excited." He props a pillow behind one shoulder. "I'm guessing Mrs. Lyght said the word *Rome* and that was all you needed to hear."

I bow my head, but not enough to hide my smile or a small nod. He's not far off.

"I just . . ." He swallows. "I want it to be everything you hope it is. I do. But I have to wonder if it actually is." Beneath the sheet, his foot rubs my knee. "Don't tense up. I have questions, that's all. You're the most important person in the world to me. If I'm going to let you go, I want to know more about it."

He's looking at me so calmly, so *rationally*. Still, the air is humming with tension and I don't think it's all from me.

"Okay," I say. I push my hair back. It's still damp, though it feels like it's been a long time since our shower. "What kind of questions?"

"For starters, what kind of internship turns up a few months before you're supposed to leave? Working at a museum, attending university there . . . it's the kind of thing people apply for years in advance and still end up on waiting lists."

"I told you—the candidate dropped out."

"And there's no qualified backup?"

"They already made other plans."

"Plans they can't change or drop for a *huge* opportunity like this?"

I take a deep breath, wanting to deflect his words but with what? "You think Mrs. Lyght is lying?"

"Of course not." He rubs a hand down my arm, which makes my skin prickle because it feels almost condescending. "But how much did she really tell you? You've told me that archaeology takes years of study. Not just a bachelor's degree—you need grad work. And yet, here you are, with no college experience. What kind of work could you do?"

"The point is that I'd be in a museum."

"For all you know, the museum could be a glorified gift shop and you'd be working the cash register."

"I'd be working a cash register in Rome."

"Exactly," he says. His voice roughens as he ticks off each point one finger at a time. "In a country where you don't know the language, the money, the customs, or the people. You really want to be uprooted? You went through all that less than a year ago. You said you never wanted to go through that again."

"Things have changed," I say. "*I've* changed."

"You really think so?" he says. "What happens when you get over there and discover you're living in a run-down dorm with ten other students and none of them speak English?"

"It's not going to be like that."

"But you don't know, do you? You hardly know anything and you're ready to fly off."

I slide my legs off the side of the bed and reach for my underwear. I'm pissed at his logic and his assumption that I'm acting irrationally, but mostly I'm pissed that he's right. "Fine," I say, tugging on my thong. "I'll go in tomorrow and talk to Mrs. Lyght."

"Good. I think that's good." I feel his hand on my back and that pisses me off, too. "You need to wait for the right opportunity, Em. Rome is always going to be there. Hell, I'll take you there myself once we graduate."

I snap my bra together and twist it into place. "It's not about a vacation."

"That's not what I meant."

"That's how it sounds." I spin to face him. "You have to remember that this is a career opportunity."

"And you'll have a lot of those, believe me."

I turn my tank right-side out and pull it over my head. I'm mad again when I wasn't going to be. "Let's wait and see what Mrs. Lyght says, okay? If she can answer all of my questions."

"Even if she does," he says, "you'd miss me as much as I'd miss you."

"I would," I say, though all I'm feeling at the moment is frustration. And irritation. "But it's nine months. We'll get through it."

His eyes cloud over. "How can you say that? This past week felt like a year."

"Because we were fighting."

"Are we fighting now?"

I sigh. I shake my head as my anger fades.

"Come here," he says gruffly.

I climb back into bed and he pulls me closer. His hand presses over my hip and his fingers find the spot where he squeezed earlier.

"Ow." I wince and he pulls away, frowning. He pushes up my tank and exposes my hip. "Oh, Em," he breathes as he runs a finger over the bruise that's already forming. "I did that, didn't I? I didn't even realize." His face pales as he looks into mine.

"It's okay."

"It's not okay. I don't want to hurt you. I would never hurt you. You know that, right?" He runs a hand over my hip, his thumb circling the bruise. It's in the shape of his finger, as if he's imprinted himself on me. "You're so delicate," he murmurs. "I can see your veins, feel your bones." He spreads his hand wide, his skin dark against my pale waist.

"I'm not that fragile."

"You are." He looks into my eyes again. "I'm trying to take care of you—to protect you—and it's like you don't see it."

"You don't need to protect me."

"Yes, I do. You're the most important thing in the world to me." Gently, he kisses the spot where I'm bruised. "That's why I'm going to keep you safe. No matter what."

He slides up beside me and holds his arms open.

I settle against his chest and let him pull me closer. I close my eyes and breathe in the smell of him, feel the press of his strong arms that have come to mean safety. I bury my face in his neck. Bury my questions in a kiss.

Bury the prickly feeling that everything is not all right.

11

"It begins again," Hannah pronounces in a voice full of doom. She holds up a cup of coffee and toasts us from her spot at the bottom of the bleachers.

Dillon and I wad up our breakfast trash as she and Spence climb up to join us. The parking lot is starting to fill and first bell will ring in about ten minutes. I feel a strange sense of anticipation and dread. I woke early and went for a run, burning off as much nervous energy as I could before meeting Dillon here. I brought peanut butter toast and we shared it on top of the empty bleachers, the sun warming our backs, the birds circling for any dropped crumbs. Now Hannah and Spence are here, clomping up the bleachers, and I'm glad for the distraction.

Spence and Dillon smack palms in greeting as Spence shoots me a smile.

"How was Disneyland?" I ask.

"Shitty," he says. "Literally. My little brother had the

stomach flu the whole week. My dad's got it now." He sits on the top bench and rests his elbows on the rail. In a white tee and long board shorts, with his blond hair dipping over one eye, he already looks like a San Diego college boy. "So what exciting things happened here?"

For a second I freeze, Rome hovering on the tip of my tongue. *Do I bring it up? What do I say?*

"Nothing," Dillon says, smoothly covering up my awkward pause. "Except that Emma missed me. Desperately," he adds with a cocky grin.

I bat my eyelashes. "Did you go somewhere?"

Spence laughs.

"Where's Jace?" Hannah asks.

"I thought I'd see him at the trail this morning, but he didn't show up," I say.

"He texted," Dillon says. "Woke up late."

"Gawd," Hannah says suddenly. "Is that Nick Walters?"

We all swivel to look behind the bleachers. Nick's long hair is mostly gone, just enough left so you can see a smiley face outlined in the white of his scalp.

"That's unsettling," Hannah says.

"Eyes in the back of his head," Spence intones in a spooky voice, and Hannah smacks him and shivers.

"Remember Dorcas?" Dillon asks.

I frown. "You didn't really know someone named Dorcas, did you?"

But Dillon doesn't hear me because Hannah's already grabbed his arm. "That was spring break, too, wasn't it? Maybe there's a weird hair thing in the universe."

Spence's grin widens. "That blue—"

"Even her toes," Dillon adds.

The three of them bust up. Awkwardly, I smile. "What?"

But before the word is even out, first bell rings. Automatically, we all get to our feet.

Hannah exchanges one more smile with Dillon. "Never mind," she says to me. "You had to be there."

I nod and try not to notice that she seems glad I wasn't.

Mrs. Lyght is straightening a stack of papers when I knock on her open door after school. She glances up and adjusts her glasses. "Emma, there you are. Come on in."

I came here directly from chemistry, so the hallways are still full of kids heading home or making their way to club meetings and practices. My heart is beating so fast you'd think I'd run all the way here.

I didn't want to squeeze in a talk before first-period history class, so I asked if we could meet now. But I'm so nervous. I want her to have the answers to my questions, but I'm afraid to ask.

"Have a seat," she says.

I nod. The back of my neck feels warm even though Mrs. Lyght's room is in one of the coolest parts of the building. The only downside is that it's also close to the cafeteria, so it always has the faint scent of tomato.

History doesn't smell like pasta sauce. It smells like the earth. Like dust and dark mud and cool sand. It smells like my first dig at an ancient Indian settlement in northern Arizona—all sunshine and sweat and mystery.

Mrs. Lyght sets some papers in a basket on her desk, then

sits and looks up at me expectantly. "So," she says. "You've thought about it?"

I smile. "For a minute or two."

She smiles back. "And?"

"And I still love the idea," I begin. "I'm waiting for a call from the study abroad office at ASU, but it looks like I meet all the qualifications for the American University. I would need a recommendation letter," I add, giving her a hopeful look.

"I'd be happy to," she says. "And if you're selected for the internship, Dr. Abella will speak to the admissions office on your behalf."

"Oh." I nod. "That's great. Then it seems like it's all . . . possible."

"But?" Mrs. Lyght asks.

I blush. "How did you know there's a but?"

"You've had a week to think about it, Emma. You must have questions."

"Actually, I do." I look above her desk to the poster hanging there. *Those who do not remember the past are condemned to repeat it.*

"Fire away," she says.

I slide my hands under my thighs to keep them from shaking. "First of all, I don't know anything about the museum."

"Bernadetta Musea," she says. "It's very small. It mainly houses the collection of an old Italian family, though they've just received a new bequest that Dr. Abella is especially excited about."

Goose bumps tiptoe up my arms. "That sounds very cool."

"It is," she says. "I'd refer you to the website, but there

isn't one. Not yet. Right now the collection is housed in a renovated school building and Dr. Abella has some very unique ideas for ways to expand."

"So if I were to go, would I be doing actual museum work?"

She frowns. "Meaning?"

"I wouldn't be working in a gift shop or taking admission tickets?"

"I promise you it won't be that. But not all the work you do will be wildly exciting. It will most likely be research, cataloguing entries—that sort of thing. But it will be skilled, meaningful work."

"Then why would Dr. Abella choose someone like me? Why not a college student with more education and experience?"

"That may be the direction he goes," she says matter-of-factly. I blush. I'm speaking as if it's already mine. "But you have a few things in your favor."

"My dad, you mean?"

"The Lorde name doesn't hurt. But I wouldn't have recommended you if I didn't think you had the passion and the ability. You have experience at dig sites and some basic knowledge of dealing with artifacts. Most college students can't match you there. Your research skills need some work, granted, but you're a talented writer, and I think it's important that you have a particular interest in the general area."

I let out a long breath. "It would be nice if I knew more about current-day Rome. The language, the money, that sort of thing."

"Does that worry you?"

"Not me," I say.

When her eyebrows quirk, I feel like I have to explain. "My boyfriend thinks I might be miserable going away for so long."

"Dillon Hobbs, right?"

I nod.

"He may be right. You wouldn't be the first student to go abroad and find the culture shock and the distance very difficult to handle."

"Then you're saying I wouldn't like it?"

"I'd never presume to tell you what you would or wouldn't like." Her eyes narrow. "I shouldn't think you'd let anyone else decide that for you, either."

Another flush burns up my neck. "No, I . . ." Swallowing, I nod. She's right. I can't be sure how I'll feel, and yes, there's a buzz of nervousness in the pit of my stomach. But enough to pass on this opportunity? I run my hands up the sides of my face and push back the hair that's fallen over my eyes. "How do I apply?"

Mrs. Lyght grins as she rolls back her chair and opens the bottom drawer of her desk. She pulls out a large brown envelope and hands it to me. "This is all the information you need. You should fill out the online application today so Dr. Abella knows you're applying. You'll also need to submit a resume."

"What about the assignment?" I ask.

"It's in there." She gestures to the envelope. "He wanted to provide actual photos so everyone has the same print quality.

You'll understand when you take a look. Just be sure to have the assignment completed and submitted to me via email a week from next Monday."

"So I have two weeks?"

She nods. "All the applicants are being given the same amount of time."

"And when will Dr. Abella decide?"

"Quickly, I'm sure. Whoever is selected needs time to plan and prepare. I would guess no more than a week or two. You should know before the end of April."

"So soon." The envelope suddenly feels heavier in my hands.

Mrs. Lyght stands and I do the same, shrugging my pack over my shoulder.

"I really hope you'll apply," she says.

I grip the envelope tighter as I realize that I do, too.

The library is busier than I expect—every computer is taken—but the couch near the printers is empty and I sit at one end, avoiding the butt print that sags in the middle of the cushion and balancing the sealed envelope on my knees. My mouth feels dry. The envelope isn't very thick. It's bent at one corner and there's a stain that looks like a thumbprint on the flap. Not very impressive for something with the power to change my future.

This makes me think of Lauren. I imagine her flashing her green eyes at me with impatience. *It's just an envelope. You're the only one with the power to change your future.* I don't know what Marissa would think. I haven't even told her about it yet. I forgot to call again yesterday, which I only remembered today during chemistry. I braved Mr. Sean's anger and pulled out my phone long enough to send a text and ask her to call.

I pry open the flap and pull out a small stack of papers.

The cover sheet has the logo of the Bernadetta Musea followed by a description of the internship and requirements.

DATES: August 28, 2017–June 8, 2018

The candidate will assist the museum director and staff in cataloguing artifacts and updating the database and other such tasks. The student will work fifteen (15) hours a week.

I skim past a paragraph on scheduling and financial information. I'm responsible for tuition, books, and room and board. I'll receive six credit hours, a small stipend, free admission to all local historical sites, and the opportunity to visit and work at local dig sites.

I read that part again and wonder if that includes Pompeii. My heart thumps hard against my ribs, and I close my eyes while the images play through my mind. I'm not a complete idiot. I realize I'm not going to show up at Pompeii and suddenly uncover something major that's been missed by hundreds of crews working on this exact location for hundreds of years. But that hasn't stopped me from imagining it so many times that I can feel the ache in my thighs from crouching in the dust, the heat of the Italian sun on my back. I can see my hand smoothing dirt and ash off something smooth and flat and discovering the diary of my fresco girl.

The first time I saw Fresco Girl, I was at Dad's office thumbing through a book of artwork discovered in Pompeii. As the villas were excavated, archaeologists found beautifully painted frescoes covering the walls. Many have been restored now, and it's amazing to look at the vivid colors of gold and red and green. One of the scenes in the book depicted a proud family gathered beneath a tree while slaves laid out a feast and provided shade. Fresco Girl was one of the slaves. She's serving a platter of fish, but her expression suggests she's somewhere far away. And her smile . . . her smile is what first caught my attention. I don't know if it's happy or sad. It's an in-between smile, like she has a secret and doesn't yet know if it's something to be glad about or not.

I made a copy of the fresco and named the girl Anna. I still imagine digging up her diary and reading about whatever it was that made her smile like that. What would she have written about those last days? Those last moments?

Lauren thinks the whole thing is morbid.

When I was six, she told me it wasn't treasure archaeologists dig up. It was dead bodies. She said buried twigs were fingers that would crawl up my neck and choke me to death. I ran sobbing to Dad. Lauren got in trouble and I got a trip downtown to the Pueblo Grande Ruins, the site of a Hohokam village. Dad explained how everything tells a story about the people who lived before us. The houses they built. The pottery they made and the baskets they wove. And yes, even their bones. He knelt beside me in the dirt and promised that the people didn't want to hurt us. They wanted me to find them so I could bring them back to life by sharing their story with the world.

That's the day I decided to be an archaeologist.

My dream never changed, though it shifted over time. Then last year, I couldn't look beyond what was happening at home. As a junior, I should have been researching colleges around the country. Instead, I was riding the roller coaster of a dad who had moved across town and started drinking and a mom who said she loved us but didn't act like it. School had become a hated place where I worried about running into my mother's lover every time I walked the halls. At first, no one knew except Marissa—at least there was that. The affair had started over the summer while Mom was overseeing new paint and carpet in the teachers' lounge. The truth didn't leak out until close to the holidays, when Dad moved out. By then I was better at hiding my emotions in front of other people. Still, I couldn't focus. I was cold all the time. Jumpy. I was waiting for the other shoe to drop, but I'd never seen the first one coming. Weekends were spent with Dad in his rental house with bare walls and a table with two place mats.

Time slipped away from me. So did my dreams of working abroad. But they're here again, dropped into my lap. Literally. I have the same fluttery feeling I get when I'm reconstructing something and I suddenly see how the pieces fit.

"Hey."

Startled, I clutch the papers to my chest and look up. "Jace!"

He smiles and dumps his heavy backpack on the floor beside me. His hair is still damp, the brown waves tousled as if he finger-combed it and called it good. Which I'm sure he did. "Baseball practice is already over?"

"It's after five."

Surprised, I hit the power button on my phone. I turned it off when I got to the library and now I see that it's 5:08 and I've missed two texts from Dillon and a call from Marissa.

"Crap. Guess I've been daydreaming."

"About what?"

I take a deep breath. "You have a minute?"

"This sounds promising." He drops down beside me, sitting sideways, and throws one arm over the back of the couch.

"Give me a sec to text Dillon." Quickly I type:

At library. Call you later.

Then I set down my phone and turn to Jace. "Mrs. Lyght is recommending me for an internship next year. In Rome."

He blinks, straight-faced. "Rome, Ohio? How exciting."

"Idiot," I say.

"Ohhhh." He nods as if he's just figured it out. "You mean the city with all the old buildings?"

"You're seething with jealousy, aren't you?"

"I only seethe on Tuesdays. But I do hate you right now." Then his lips quirk and his right cheek dimples. I was right about Jace from the beginning—he is the kind of guy who smiles a lot. Jace is cute in a messy way—wavy hair the color of a paper bag, wrinkled T-shirts and worn jeans. His nose is crooked and a little smushed from running into a stop sign on a skateboard when he was ten. It's his sense of humor and his easy smile that make so many girls call him *adorable*. That and the dimples. "So tell me," he says. "What happened? What did she say? When do you leave?"

It all comes out in a rush and I feel myself getting excited all over again. Especially when Jace's eyes widen and the smartest guy I know is reduced to words like *What? Wow!*

Jace has turned out to be one of my closest friends—and not just because of Dillon. Our morning trail runs started by accident, but now we try to meet up at least two days a week. It's not as if we bare our hearts at seven a.m., but you get to know someone when you spend time together like that.

"If you go to Rome, you'll be within spitting distance of Pompeii," Jace says.

Of course his brain goes to the same place mine did. Jace has a thing for doomed cities, just like me. I'm fascinated by the history—he's fascinated by natural disasters. Suddenly I realize that this internship would be perfect for him, too. Jace is crazy smart at just about everything and loves history almost as much as I do. "I'm kind of surprised Mrs. Lyght didn't ask you," I say as I think about it. My chest tightens with an uncomfortable thought. "You think it's just because of my dad?"

"No way. She wouldn't risk her reputation recommending someone who couldn't handle it."

I nod, feeling a little easier. "And she wouldn't offer it to you because you're already a Bergen Scholar."

He smiles, but it's forced. I know Jace well enough to recognize the sudden tightness in his shoulders.

"What?"

He shifts the backpack by his leg. "I would love for five minutes to go by without someone bringing that up."

"Why?" I ask. "It's a good thing."

"But it's not everything."

"What does that mean?"

"Nothing. Never mind."

I narrow my eyes. "What's going on? You've been so quiet. Even Dillon thinks—"

"I know what Dillon thinks, okay?" he snaps.

I stiffen. Jace flushes and looks away. I don't think I've ever heard him pissed off before.

"Sorry," he mutters, and ruffles his hair with nervous fingers. "It's just turned into this big deal."

"It is a big deal." The Bergen Scholar is gifted every year to a student with remarkable potential. As long as Jace chooses an in-state university, the scholarship pays for tuition, books, a full year of study abroad, and a $500 stipend each semester. Plus, it's like a banner on your resume screaming, *Hire Me, Hire Me*.

"I don't know if it's what I want."

I blink, not sure I heard him. "What isn't what you want? The scholarship? The money?"

He shifts on the couch so he's facing out, his long legs angled wide, his hands rubbing the faded denim of his jeans. "All of it," he says. "College."

My mouth hangs open; I have no words. My brain feels blank. If anyone is made for college, it's Jace. "When did this happen?"

"It's something I've been thinking about for a while."

"For a while? Why didn't you say something?"

"To Dillon?" He gives me a pointed look and I hate to admit it, but I know what he's thinking. In Dillon's mind it's all settled. Jace will take the scholarship and go to ASU. They'll play club baseball and study together and we'll all go to Pizza Joe's every Friday night. No wonder Jace has been acting weird all spring when the subject of next year comes up.

"You could have told me," I say.

"I've wanted to. I thought you'd worry for Dillon's sake."

"Probably. But I'd also be happy for yours. If it's what you really want."

He shrugs. "I'm still trying to figure that out. Before I say anything to Dillon."

I nod, but then I'm startled into a gasp as a new thought

fills my mind. It's as if I've just rubbed dirt off a flat rock and found a coin instead.

"This helps explain it," I say. "Why Dillon has been acting . . . funny."

"Funny how?"

"I told him about the internship and he wasn't happy," I say. "I knew he wouldn't like the idea of me leaving, but then he got . . . angry." One hand curves around my stomach and it takes me a second to realize I'm feeling for the bruised spot on my hip. "But he must have known that something's going on with you, too."

Jace sighs. "He doesn't get it. He's where he wants to be. The future is all laid out and it's exactly how he wants it."

"But it's not what you want?"

"I want to see the world."

"You don't have to go to ASU," I say. "You could give up the Bergen and get a scholarship just about anywhere."

"But I'd still be staring at a screen all day or buried in a book. I want to discover things for myself, you know?" He tilts his head and pins me with his deep brown eyes. "Don't you?"

The papers are in my lap. It's hard to express just how much I truly want to go. This past year I've carefully constructed a full-color picture of a future here, being with Dillon, working at local dig sites, eventually getting a job teaching. And it's a great future. But now the picture is flickering in and out of focus as if it's not as solid as I'd imagined. As if there might be another picture forming just beyond it.

A picture I want to see.

"Don't feel guilty, Emma."

My gaze lifts, surprised. Jace is always smiling, always so funny. Now his eyes are serious. "This internship is perfect for you. You've got to take it."

"What about Dillon?"

"He'll accept it. What else is he going to do? Break up with you?" He shakes his head. "Never going to happen."

"That sounds so selfish." But the hope is a breathless feeling in my chest. Jace is right. If I get in, Dillon will have to handle the separation. "It's not a guarantee," I say, reminding myself along with Jace. "I still have to complete a project."

"What project?"

"I don't know," I admit. "It's in the packet."

"That packet?" His eyes widen. "Well, what are you waiting for?"

I laugh. "Someone kind of interrupted me."

"What kind of idiot would do that?" He gestures to the papers in my hand. "Come on. Let's see."

"Don't you have work to do?"

"Yeah," he says. "Researching pulleys for a physics project. This sounds way more interesting."

As I flip the page, my phone vibrates beside me. Glancing down at the screen, I see another text from Dillon.

Have a surprise. Meet me at your house

Quickly, I type.

Later. Still working. Love you.

Then I flutter the papers and smile at Jace. "You ready?"

13

It's on the final page of the packet. A single sheet labeled INTERNSHIP ASSIGNMENT. I tilt the paper so Jace can read it with me.

Today's museum patron is looking for a richer experience. More than verifiable facts, they want to understand artifacts within the context of culture and civilization. At Bernadetta Musea, we provide visitors with a uniquely satisfying experience by creating stories that bring our collection to life.

In that spirit, you will choose one of the two items pictured below and create a narrative history. You will combine historical fact with a fictionalized account of who might have used the item and how.

In addition, provide a traditional catalog entry for *both* items, including all relevant facts. Final submission should include the following:

1. Traditional catalog entry for each item.
2. An essay on one item of no more than 2,000 words.

My heart races as I read it over again. "He wants me to make up a story?" I glance at Jace. "How freaking cool is that?"

"Look at the items," Jace says.

One is a coin, pictured both front and back, though it's difficult to see much detail because the coin has been worn down. The second is a ring, and I gasp when I see the design: a serpent's head. "They found bracelets at Pompeii decorated with serpents."

Jace grabs the paper. "You think this was from Pompeii?"

"I don't know," I say. "Probably not, but that doesn't matter." I blink, trying to focus my thoughts. "If it's from the same time period, I could make it work."

"What do you mean?"

"I could write my essay about the last hours of Pompeii. About this ring and the person who owned it."

"What person?" he asks. "You'd make up someone?"

I think back to the fresco, to Anna, to the face of the slave girl. I may not find her diary, but I can bring her back to life after all. "I know somebody," I say. "Somebody who lived in Pompeii."

He stares at me as if he's wondering whether I'm on heavy medication. "I have no idea what that means," he says. "But it's weird and I like it."

I grin. "I like it, too."

My phone vibrates. Irritated, I look at the screen.

"Crap," I say.

"Dillon?"

I collect the pages and slide them back into the envelope. "I've got to go."

"You know, I might be able to help you with the coin."

"Yeah? How?"

"I've got some coin catalogs at home. I can check this against it."

"Coin catalogs? From ancient civilizations?"

He lets his mouth drop open. "You mean not everyone has a set?" Then he shrugs. "I went through a pirate phase when I was younger. Pretending I had one eye wasn't all that fun, but treasure chests filled with gold coins captured my imagination. One thing led to another." He gestures to the copy machine. "Mind if I make a copy?"

"You kidding? Go for it."

I sling my pack over my shoulder and hand him the papers. As the machine hums and whirs, I can't help bouncing on my toes I'm so excited. Jace's smile turns to an indulgent grin as he hands me the originals. "Get out of here," he says. "Try not to float into any walls on your way out."

I laugh, pressing the envelope to my heart as I let the amazing truth sink in.

I'm really doing this.

Dillon is parked in front of my house when I pull into the garage. His black Ford pickup gleams in the late-afternoon sun. He waxes it himself twice a month, which, it turns out, is a very sexy thing to watch. I leave my pack in the car and head down the drive. He's leaning against the passenger door looking extremely yummy in a baby-blue tee and fitted black jeans.

"I was at the library," I say.

"I know, I'm sorry." He pulls an envelope from his back pocket. "But I have something for us. Something you'll like."

I smile and reach for the envelope. He lifts it out of my reach and instead grabs me for a quick, soft kiss. He pulls back, his hand still around my waist as he rocks me in the vee of his legs. "Your hair smells like Doritos."

"Library couch."

"Must have been the one by the printers."

"Only one open."

He hands me the envelope. It's unsealed, and inside are two tickets.

LOVE THROUGH THE AGES is printed in curly script on the front. "You got our prom tickets!"

He smiles. "Will you be my love through the ages?"

"Me and my Dorito hair would be honored." I study the tickets, rubbing them between my fingers. We've talked about prom before, about going, so it's not as if it's a surprise. But still. I'm a little embarrassed about how excited I am. "I'd given up on the idea of ever going to a prom."

"Why?" he asks.

"I didn't go my junior year and then I moved here." I smile up at him. "I figured everyone would already be paired up and I'd be the lonely new girl watching Nicholas Sparks movies on prom night."

"But you'd met me by then."

"Yeah, and I couldn't tell if you were flirting with me or just being nice."

He grins and tugs me until I lose my balance and fall against his chest. "All part of my master plan."

"Quit," I giggle. "My dad is inside." I push against his chest and right myself, but I curl one finger through a belt loop. "I never told you this, but I used to get jealous when you guys talked about prom. And I still don't know the real story about last year."

"What do you mean?" he asks.

By this time last March, I was spending every weekend at my dad's and Saturday mornings at Cupz pretending not to like Dillon as much I did. Jace was usually there, sometimes Spence and sometimes Hannah. I'd heard them talk about prom and Dillon made a point to tell me they were all going as a group, but I'd always wondered.

"Was it really a group thing?" I ask, trying to read the expression in his eyes. "Nobody paired off? Nobody wanted to pair off?"

"It wasn't like that," he says. "We were all friends."

Hannah showed me a picture once and I couldn't get over the guys—Dillon, Jace, and Spence—all in suits and bow ties. But mostly I studied the girls. Hannah, of course, and Lydia, who I'd met once at Cupz before she moved to Ohio with her family. The third girl was Alayna Diaz. I don't know her very well—she's a year younger than us—but Mr. Diaz, the baseball coach, is her father, so she's at most of the games. I always assumed Dillon had asked her to go, maybe because of that connection.

I tug at his belt loop. "So you didn't buy someone a corsage? Arrange to pick them up? Like maybe Alayna?" I tug again so he knows I'm not giving up.

"Not Alayna," he finally says. He doesn't blush easily, but I swear his cheeks darken as he admits, "Hannah."

"Hannah?" My voice rises at least an octave.

"It was a group thing, like I said."

"But Hannah? I wouldn't have thought . . ." My words trail off. With all the things she's dropped hints about, she's never once mentioned prom. What does that mean? Is she carrying a torch for Dillon? I feel like I just drank milk way past its expiration date. I wind another finger through his belt loop, tightening my hold. "Should I be jealous?"

"No!" He says it flatly with a sense of finality that makes me feel good.

"What about Spence?"

"Spence went with Alayna. It was before him and Hannah." Dillon rolls his eyes. "It sounds like a made-for-TV movie. It was just something to do. This year, with you, it's going to be special."

"That kind of talk is going to get you a kiss." I fit my mouth over his bottom lip and nip at him with my teeth.

"Mmmm," he murmurs. "What's it going to take to get a kiss in other places?"

"You mean places other than the sidewalk outside my house?"

He laughs. "I love you, Dorito Girl." He brushes his lips over mine and then kisses the ticklish spot near my temple. I swat him with the tickets and he takes the envelope, sliding it into his back pocket. "The others are going to want to do a group thing again, but I want to do prom just the two of us. Something special."

"We can always meet the others for pictures beforehand," I suggest. "Hannah and I are going to shop for dresses this weekend. I'll bring it up with her then."

"Perfect. You're perfect." He plants a kiss on the tip of my nose. "So what were you doing at the library?"

I run my tongue over suddenly dry lips. "I was going over the application from Mrs. Lyght."

His eyes darken. "The application?"

I rub his forearms, wanting to soothe him with my touch if I can't with my words. "I asked her all of your questions and a few of my own."

"Let me guess, she had all the answers."

"Maybe because there are answers," I say carefully. My sandals wobble on the curve of the gutter as I step back.

"Maybe," he says. But his tight jaw says he doesn't believe it.

"You'll feel better about it when I tell you more. This guy, Dr. Abella, he sounds really cool. I'll show you the assignment. It's so interesting! I get to—"

"You're doing an assignment?" he interrupts.

I look at the gray pavement and then up to a sky that's deepening to an even darker gray. "Yeah, I told you. I have to apply."

"And you'll have your dad to help you. How convenient."

"I'm not going to ask my dad for help." I frown, not wanting to fight about this again but his words rub at my pride. "You don't think I'm good enough?"

"Of course I think you're good enough," he says impatiently. "Don't you see the connection?"

"What connection?"

"Mrs. Lyght offers you this thing. Mrs. Lyght is a friend of your dad's. Your dad has always wanted you to go away for college."

"He wanted me to go to U of A so I'd be close to Lauren."

"Or so you'd be farther away from me?"

"No. Dillon. You're reading way too much into this. That's crazy."

His shoulders go back. "You think I'm crazy?"

"No." I swallow a hot breath. "Can we stop arguing about this?"

"Sure," he snaps. "Whatever you want." The anger in his

eyes makes me take another step back. What's going on? This isn't like Dillon. I don't know how to talk to him when he's like this.

Forcing my voice lower, softer, I say, "I have two weeks to finish the assignment and then another week or two to hear if I'm even in the running. Can we wait until then to fight?" I'm trying to be funny but he doesn't even crack a smile.

"Perfect," he says. "Right around prom. It can ruin that, too."

With a sharp movement that startles me, his elbow rockets back and slams into the truck. The metal hisses and vibrates, denting under the force.

"Emma?"

I spin around. Dad is standing in the drive. He's still in his work clothes, but his button-down is hanging loose over his trousers and he's barefoot.

I swallow my heart and force a smile. "Hi, Dad."

"Everything okay out here?"

"Yeah." I can hardly hear myself over the scream of my blood. "Fine."

"You want to stay for dinner, Dillon?"

Dillon's smile is icy. A chill runs up my spine. His voice is low and controlled as he says, "That's nice of you, Mr. Lorde. Very nice. But I'd better get home."

He turns back to me and his eyes are flat and distant. "I'll see you later."

I stand back as he climbs into his truck and slams the door. A second later, the truck roars to life. I watch him drive off and feel myself shake in reaction. It all happened so fast. And it's dusk—it's not easy to see clearly; the dent might have been a trick of my eyes.

I press my arms to my sides, my hands to my chest. If I can get my heart to stop thundering, maybe I can convince myself it didn't happen at all.

It is raining gray.

It began a few hours ago. The black smoke and fumes rose high enough to kiss the feet of the gods and then the gray pebbles began to fall.

The sky is falling!

Even now Anna hears the screams that tear through the dark day. There are those in Pompeii who still remember the mountain erupting seventeen years earlier. They are rushing toward roads and the seaport, taking as much as they can carry.

Anna longs to run with them.

"The pebbles are nothing to fear," Marcus tells her. "They cannot hurt us here."

Marcus has brought her to his family home. His parents are visiting relatives in Misenum and the home is vacant but for the household slaves, and many of them have fled. She and Marcus are standing in the atrium as the world showers down around them. "We must go," Anna says.

Marcus stares up at the sky, worry creasing his forehead.

"My father," he says. "He left me the responsibility. I cannot leave the house unprotected from looters. Besides," he tells her, "the villa is strongly built. We will be safe waiting out the storm here."

So Anna silences the uneasy voice in her head, concentrating on Marcus's words.

At first he is right. The pebbles are light in color and weight. But they continue to fall.

Beyond the walls of Marcus's home, the pebbles are now an ocean three feet deep that flows down the streets. Families fight the current toward the city gates while even now the atrium is flooded with stone, the rectangular pool bubbling strangely. When the great statue of Jupiter crashes from its pedestal, it is Marcus who cries out.

"The jewels," he says. "The family crest. I must carry them with us."

"No," Anna cries. "There is no time!" But Marcus has already disappeared into the villa's corridor. Panic pushes her toward the door. She should go. She must go! But indecision and fear hold her like iron shackles. She will wait five more minutes. Just five more.

Eight minutes later, Marcus returns with a wooden chest tucked under one arm.

"Thank the gods!" she cries. There is time—if they hurry.

From outside, a great roar fills the air as if the sun and the moon have crashed to the earth.

An instant later, the ceiling above them buckles.

The Web page calls it "a decorative motif."

I call it beyond creepy and the coolest thing I've ever seen.

The Capuchin Crypt is in Rome—where else—and doesn't just hold the remains of friars. It's decorated with them. The walls are layered with decayed bones. The chandeliers are shriveled skeleton heads dangling from bleached femurs and fibulas.

This is what he wants me to give up?

It's been hours since Dillon drove off and I'm still shaking over the whole thing. My Rome research is supposed to be a distraction, and mostly it's working. I stumbled onto this website searching for religious motifs. I shudder again at the words engraved on a sign in the crypt:

What you are, we once were.

What we are, you someday will be.

It's a reminder, as the friars meant it to be, that life is short.

Exactly. I wish I could show this to Dillon. I wish I could call him right now, except that I'm too pissed to share anything with him.

SORRY

he texted a while ago.

Me too

I texted back.

I'm not sure what I'm sorry about. That he got so mad? That he tried to put an elbow through his truck door? That I just found the most awesome site and I can't share it with my boyfriend because he's too busy coming up with conspiracy theories to listen?

My phone beeps with a new text. I sigh and dig the cell out of the folds of my comforter. *Now what?*

But it isn't Dillon. It's Jace. I relax as I read.

Found a coin in my book with a similar back. The woman may be Faustina, wife of Marcus Aurelius

Should I have heard of her?

Said to have ordered deaths, instigated revolt, and slept with gladiators.

And they put her on a coin?

Gotta love those Romans

I pause to reply because I'm laughing.

Thx. Will check Dad's database.

I'll keep looking more tomorrow

This is where being the daughter of Dr. David Lorde comes in handy. As a professor, he has access to ASU's huge online library system, which means I also have access. I'm not sure who else is applying for the internship, but the database is a definite advantage for me.

I set the laptop on my bed, unfold my legs, and stretch. I can feel how late it is in the stiffness of my shoulders and back. I'm already wearing the tank top and boxers that I sleep in. My teeth are brushed, my face is washed and moisturized, and my hair is brushed out. Normally I sleep with it loose, but I had to pull it back in a pony because I keep twisting it, and every time I twist, I'm reminded of why I'm in such a . . . twisty mood.

Hair out of sight, Dillon's flying elbow out of mind.

The living room lights are dimmed, and at first I'm not sure it's him. "Dad?"

He's a shape on the couch, but as soon as I speak, he shifts into a more upright position, murmurs, "Hmmmm?" and blinks owlishly.

"Why don't you go to bed?"

"Just about to," he says. He clicks on the lamp on the table beside the couch. The memory book is sitting there, along with a half-full glass of wine.

"What are you doing?" he asks.

"Some research for my application."

"Is this the assignment you told me about at dinner?"

I nod. "Do you mind if I use your computer?"

"You want to access the library?"

"I think I know who's on the coin. I want to check it out."

"Of course, baby."

I start for his office but then find myself slowing down, Dillon's voice echoing in my head. My pulse skips.

No, he didn't. He wouldn't.

But . . .

My feet turn and take me back to where I'm not sure I really want to be. Hesitantly, I rest a hand on the worn leather chair facing Dad. "Can I ask you something?"

He rubs a hand over his face. "About your research?"

"About the internship. You didn't have anything to do with it, right? I mean, you didn't use your influence to get Mrs. Lyght to ask me, did you?"

"It wasn't *influence*," he says.

It feels like I've swallowed a brick. *Oh my God.* I sink onto the arm of the chair, my research forgotten. "You knew about it?" I choke out. "Before I came home and told you . . . you knew?"

"Well, yes, but—"

"You acted surprised!"

"I didn't. You were excited and I let you tell me your wonderful news."

I scrub my fingers through my hair, yanking strands of it from the rubber band. "Dillon was right," I breathe. "You arranged this."

He looks bewildered. "All I did was make a suggestion. You were the obvious choice."

I'm so angry that tears scald the corners of my eyes. "How could you?"

"It's a fabulous opportunity. I did it for you."

"Because you want me to go to Rome or because you want me away from Dillon?"

"Baby—"

"Don't 'baby' me! I'm in love with Dillon. You know that."

"You don't know what love is," he says. "You're barely eighteen."

"What does that mean?" I throw my hands wide. "Are people my age incapable of love? Is there a certain age when I'll suddenly wake up and be able to experience that emotion? When is it, Dad? You want to tell me? Because I really don't know."

"Emma—"

"No!" I snap, anger pouring out in waves I can't begin to contain. "I'm sorry I'm so young, and if I could have waited another few years to meet Dillon, then yeah, I would have. But it didn't happen that way. We met when I was seventeen and we fell in love, and it's every bit as real as if we were twenty-five or thirty or four flipping hundred!"

He blinks slowly in time with the shake of his head. "You don't know what's real at this age. It's all hormones and crushes and exploration."

"Oh, please." I cross my arms over my chest. "Then how can I love you, right?" I give him the same professorial quirk of my eyebrows that he likes to give me. "I mean, I'm only a *child*."

"That's not romantic love. It's not the same thing."

"Why isn't it?" I demand. "Because you say so?"

"I'm only saying that a separation wouldn't be the worst thing."

"For who?" I snap. "For you? How could you do this?"

"I don't understand why you're so upset." He looks honestly confused.

I want to scream. Dillon and I fought over this—and *Dillon was right!* I slide his wineglass toward him, the deep purple liquid sloshing against the crystal.

"Here, Dad, drink up. At least this you understand."

16

Dillon is waiting when I come outside the next morning.

During the fall, he picked me up every day, but since baseball has been in full swing, he has practice after school and I usually drive myself. But today we need to talk.

The sky is a cloudless blue, the air fragrant from the thick hedge blooming next door. I breathe in the morning, trying to relax as I walk down the drive. The truck windows are tinted, so I can't see inside. Is he watching me? Is he thinking about the door the way I am? He's popped the dent out, so I can only see a slight indent, and only because the sun is shining in just the right way.

I picture him working on it last night. He would've been mad, the way I was. Is he still? I'm wearing a shirt I know he likes—red, sleeveless, ribbed over my stomach, and tucked into jean shorts with a red corded belt. I wore it for the first time on Valentine's Day. That was a good night.

The door pops open and Dillon is leaning across my seat. He's not mad. I can see that right away. Wary, maybe. Unsure. We both have things to be sorry for.

"Hey," he says as I climb in.

"Hi." I close the door and face him in the shaded coolness of the truck. He meets my gaze with a hesitant smile and then reaches behind his seat and lifts up a white bakery bag. I don't need to read the logo to recognize it's from Doe's Donuts, my favorite. A sudden heat presses against my eyes as a laugh rises in my throat. I unzip my backpack and pull out a bag of my own.

When I hold it up, his eyes get a little shiny. "You baked?"

"Blueberry muffins."

He smiles and wiggles his bag. "Chocolate long john with sprinkles. Otherwise known as Apology Donut."

He hands me the bag and takes the one I hold out. I open the waxy edges and breathe in the smell of fresh-baked chocolate. He's doing the same, sniffing the still-warm muffins.

"When did you have time?" he asks.

"I couldn't sleep."

He kisses me, his mouth so gentle that when he pulls away, I'm as melty as the chocolate frosting.

"I'm sorry," I say.

He rests his forehead against mine. "So am I."

"I still think you overreacted," I begin.

"Emma—"

"But you were right," I add before he can say more.

He pulls back, his eyes searching mine.

"My dad did know about it. He . . . suggested Mrs. Lyght recommend me for the internship."

His eyes darken three shades from night to stormy night. "I *knew* it. That goddamn—"

"Dillon," I say sharply. "He's my dad."

"And he's trying to break us up."

"He's not going to." I put my hand on his chest just above his heart. "Only we can do that."

"And we're not—"

"Ever."

He lets out a deep breath. "Then tell him and Mrs. Lyght exactly where to shove this internship."

Next door, Mr. French is backing out in his white sedan. He waves at me through the windshield. I wave back, smiling as if everything is just perfect. Dillon drums his fingers on the steering wheel. I watch the car drive off as I say, "It's still a great opportunity."

"Are you kidding me?"

I lock gazes with him. "My dad's reasons for doing it were wrong. I told him that, too, and I told him that I love you and he needs to respect that. But it's still an amazing internship."

Dillon twists his hand over the wheel so tightly it makes a squeaky sound. "He wins?"

"No!" I say. "*I* win. I get Rome for a year and you forever." I dip my head to follow the drop of his gaze. "Dillon, come on. Why can't you see what this means to me?" I hold my breath, hoping. *Hoping* . . .

The sun skims the edge of his cheek. There's a thin triangle of stubble on his jaw where he missed shaving. The sight makes my breath catch. He's always so careful but this is affecting him as much as it is me. This is love. This is why we're going to be okay.

He lets out a long breath. "I'm tired is all. I didn't sleep on the cruise. I haven't slept well since I've been back."

"I haven't been sleeping much, either."

We're quiet, the engine a low hum.

"Will you at least try to understand?" I ask.

"But I need you to understand, too. Things are hard right now," he says. Dillon looks up at me, his jaw moving as if he's chewing over some heavy emotion. "I keep picturing this old tent my dad had. We went camping a couple of times and I remember how we'd stretch out the canvas and then he'd anchor it to the ground with these heavy iron stakes and a flat-edged hammer. Four of them—one at each corner. No matter what kind of weather we had, that tent was solid." He runs a fisted hand over his thigh. "I feel like that tent, Emma. And one by one the stakes have been pulled up. You're the last stake, and if you're gone, then what's keeping me here?"

"Don't say that."

"It's how I feel." That look of panic is back in his eyes.

I lean forward so I can squeeze his arm. "I'm always going to be here for you. No matter what."

We touch foreheads again, pressing against each other. Somehow, I feel closer to him than ever.

"So what are we going to do?" he asks.

"We're not letting this come between us."

"That's what I want, too, Em."

"Okay, then."

"Okay."

We stay the way we are, just our foreheads touching while the sun creeps up a little higher on the dash.

I hate to break the spell, but we're going to be late for

school. As if he's thinking the exact same thing, he lifts his head and smiles weakly. "Then the way I see it, we have only one problem."

I tense.

"There are two muffins in this bag, and I really don't want to share."

My laugh is full of relief. "Idiot. They're both for you." I open my bakery bag and pull out my donut. We still haven't resolved things, not fully, but I feel lighter. Hopeful. As Dillon drives us to school, I sink my teeth into fresh dough and warm chocolate. Apology Donut is the best thing I've ever tasted.

17

"I like toilet paper," Hannah says. "I'm not giving it up."

"I'm not saying you have to drip dry," Jace retorts.

We're sitting at our usual lunch table outside. It's one of those round picnic tables with three curved benches and we're all in our spots as if there are nameplates. Dillon to my left, Jace next to him, Hannah to my right sharing her bench with Spence, who is already halfway through a pizza, while the rest of us have teriyaki rice bowls from the food truck that comes twice a week. Hannah also has her usual bag of pork rinds, which look as disgusting as they sound.

Jace spears a chunk of chicken with a plastic fork. "I'm just saying that if our principal wants to start an environmental program, then we should be using recycled products."

"Have you ever used recycled toilet paper?" Hannah asks.

"The toilet paper isn't recycled," Jace says.

Hannah tosses a pork rind. Dillon shoots out a hand and

catches it in midair. "Are these actually made of pork?" he asks, sniffing it suspiciously.

"It looks like a plastic shower ring," I say.

Hannah grabs the pork rind and drops it into one of the potted palms that surround the patio. "We're not talking about my lunch. We're talking about my right to little pillows of softness."

I sense a Hannah-rant on its way. This group has such a strange mix of personalities. I wouldn't have put them together, but my image of the group is still shifting—shaped by each new thing I learn. Like Dillon and Hannah going to prom last year.

Hannah shudders now as she winds herself into full drama mode. "We had reclaimed postconsumer *whatever* toilet paper at acting camp last summer, and let me tell you, one swipe and you'll know exactly what happened to the newspapers our generation stopped reading."

Spence flutters his lashes—his version of an eye roll.

"What about our landfills?" Jace asks.

Hannah dismisses that with a wave of her fork. "I don't want to hear about landfills."

"What about global warming? What about our ability to feed and clothe nine billion people while sustaining a crumbling ecosystem? What about mutated alien zombies created from too much fluoride in our water?"

"I worry about mutated alien zombies," Hannah insists. "Who doesn't? It's my ass that wants Charmin Ultra Soft."

She looks to me for support, and I have to nod.

Jace throw up his hands. "And that," he says, "is what's

wrong with our society. We'd rather save our asses than the world."

"How many rolls of Charmin do you need for nine billion people?" Spence asks.

"Extra for you," Dillon says. "Because you're full of shit."

Spence grins through a full mouth.

"Well, it's good that we have you," I tell Jace. "You'll figure out a way to stop the zombies."

He sighs. "I always have to do everything."

A siren wails from the street opposite the school and we all pause to listen. The noise quickly fades, which means no one has been caught with drugs or driven through the school fence.

"So did you tell everyone about the internship?" Jace asks me.

I feel Dillon stiffen as Hannah and Spence both say, "Internship?"

"Next year," I say. "I have a chance to work at a museum in Rome."

"Italy?" Hannah's voice rises.

"Who'd you have to sleep with to get that?" Spence asks. "The pope?"

"Fortunately," I say, "that's not my assignment." Then I explain the project. "It's all due a week from Monday, but it's a long shot."

Hannah wipes her mouth with a napkin. "When did all this come up?"

Mentally I try to relax but it's hard when I can feel Dillon so tense beside me. "Right before spring break."

"And you didn't mention it?" Hannah looks from Dillon to me.

"I wasn't sure I'd even apply until yesterday afternoon. Jace knows because he turned up at the library as I was going through the paperwork."

"But"—Hannah shakes her head—"what about next year? ASU? You and Dillon in the same dorm—I thought it was all set?"

"It was," Dillon says. "It is."

I swallow. "This just came up and it's . . ."

"Rome," Jace says, finishing my sentence for me. "This is the real deal. Emma's not going to get a chance like this more than once."

"Why not?" Hannah asks. "She's not even a college student yet. She can apply for something like this every year until she's out of grad school, right?"

"Why take that chance?" Jace counters. "The opportunity is here now."

"*Dillon* is here now," Hannah says. She exchanges a pointed look with Jace. I feel like I'm missing something, but that's the norm with Hannah. I've tried to overlook the things I don't like about her, for Dillon's sake, but I'm about ready to give up on that.

"What if you get it?" Hannah asks me.

"What do you mean?"

"I mean . . ." Hannah pauses and licks her lips. "You're just going to break up?"

"We're not breaking up," I snap. I want to smack her and tell her to shut it. Dillon and I worked it out this morning and now she's winding him back up. "We're going to Skype every day."

"For a year?"

Spence puts a hand on her arm, but she brushes it off. "Sorry," she says. "I just don't get it."

Dillon wads up his napkin and throws it in his bowl. "I've got to go."

"Wait." I gather my trash and stand. "I'll come with you."

"No. Stay," he says. There's hurt in his eyes. "See how *you* like it."

Okay, he's pissed. I get that.

Just how many different ways does he need to illustrate it?

Since Tuesday's lunch, I feel like I'm dating Mount Vesuvius. On the surface, everything is fine. In fact, that's the only word I can get out of him.

"I'm fine."

"Everything is fine."

"We're doing juuuuust fine."

But deep down, he's like a slow-boiling pit of lava. His smile is strained. His fingers are twitchy. I can see the outline of his jaw muscle, he's got it clenched so often. The only thing missing is puffs of steam coming out of his ears. And now it's Friday night and I'm starting to get pissed that he's pissed.

What happened to trying? Is this him trying?

Our study session is a waste of time—why did he invite me to the guesthouse anyway? I glare from under my eyelashes. I'm on the bed, but instead of sitting beside me as usual, Dillon's slouched in the green-striped, tall-backed chair usually reserved for dirty laundry. He's pretending to read his econ book. At least, I think he's pretending. The cinnamon candle is flickering on his nightstand. Does he think he's setting the mood for later? Because if he thinks I'm getting naked with him, he's going to be very disappointed.

I huff out a breath, forcing my gaze back to my laptop and a Wikipedia entry on Pompeii. I've also brought a library book and my assignment for the internship, but I can't focus. That's the worst part. I've wasted—*wasted*—two days that I should have been working. Other than the research Jace has done on the coin, I've made almost no headway on the ring. I've barely even gotten through my regular schoolwork. Fuming over a fuming boyfriend takes waaaaay too much energy.

Or is that his plan?

Frustrated, I huff out another breath.

He flips a page of his book. "You getting a cold or something?" he asks.

Anger bubbles. He's not the only one with hot lava churning inside him. "Oh, so now you're talking to me?"

"Don't know what you mean."

I close the lid of my laptop. "You said you were going to try."

He doesn't even look up. "I am trying."

"Then you wouldn't have let what Hannah said get to you like this."

Another page crackles as he flips it over. "How am I supposed to feel when my friend cares about me more than my girlfriend?"

That deserves another huff, which I deliver loudly. "Hannah doesn't care about you more, and of course she'd stay. She has no reason to go."

He looks up, locking his gaze with mine. "Even if she did, she wouldn't."

"Is that what you want?" I ask. "Someone who's going to follow a step behind you for the next fifty years?"

"What I want," he says, "is you. Not behind me. Not ahead of me. Right fucking beside me." He slams the book closed.

I flinch but at least we're finally talking. "Can we discuss this without getting mad?"

"Too late for that—I am mad. I don't know how to *stop* being mad." He throws the book on the ground. It skids open, the pages fluttering. "We had a whole future mapped out—the two of us—and now I'm supposed to sit around and wait to see if I'm a part of it anymore?"

"That's not what's happening. You should be happy for me. You should be helping me!"

"You want help?" His eyes narrow. He's up so suddenly, one second in the chair, the next across from me, his one hundred and eighty pounds feeling more like two thousand as the bed sags beneath his weight. He spins my library book so the title is facing him. *"Bodies from the Ash,"* he reads. "That's what you want to leave me for? A city that's been dead for two thousand years?" His gaze razors up to meet mine. "You want help? I'll help you with the ashes."

He takes the sheet of paper with my assignment. Before I realize what he's doing, he's got the candle. A small spiral of smoke follows his movement, the flame sputtering in the air as he swings the red pillar in front of himself. He holds the corner of the paper above the flame.

"Dillon, stop it!"

The paper catches fire, flares white, then blackens in a ragged line along the edge of the page.

I push up to my knees and grab his shoulder with one hand as I reach for the paper with the other. I yank it from him, then shove at his shoulder. Fury heats my breath as I blow at the curling edge of flame. It flares before dying out. The smell of smoke sticks in my throat. The bottom quarter of the sheet is burned, the serpent ring mostly gray ash. Thank God I let Jace make a copy.

My heart is pounding and I'm shaking so hard the bed is wobbling. It's all I can do to hold myself together and not give in to the sobs that threaten. "What is wrong with you?" I cry. "What are you thinking?"

He barks out a laugh that isn't anything like a laugh. "You were scared, weren't you? Your precious assignment was burning. You grabbed that paper so fast—you weren't about to let anything happen to it." He tilts his head, watching me. "What about me? Would you do the same for me? Would you save me?"

"This is crazy. I'm going." Breathing hard and fast, I gather up my things.

"Then who's going to save me?"

I swipe at the edge of one eye and the heel of my palm comes away wet with tears. "What are you talking about?"

He raises the candle again. The flickering light hollows out his face, makes his eyes look dead.

"Dillon—"

Before I can finish whispering his name, he tilts the candle and a pool of deep red wax shifts like a living thing. Then with a tiny flick of his wrist, he tips the candle and a drop of hot wax sizzles on the soft flesh of his inner wrist.

My body freezes and then begins to tremble. "Dillon. For God's sake, don't—"

Another flick of his wrist and wax begins to drop like blood. Heavy. Red. Each drop lands beside the next, his skin puckering and blistering from the heat. In the time it takes me to cry out, there's a trail of red down the line of his vein.

"Stop!" I yell. I grab the candle and he doesn't fight me. He lets it go. Lets me blow it out and set it, trembling, on the table by my side of the bed. My mouth is dry. Thick bile gathers at the back of my throat. "I'll get something for your arm."

I slide off the bed. My body feels too heavy for my legs. The carpet is rough under my bare feet as I steady myself. The lights are all on, and I can see the gleam of Dillon's weights in the next room, the outline of the bathroom. My purse is sitting on the floor where I dropped it, my sandals next to it. It's all familiar and all completely foreign. I can't feel myself in this place. In this moment. I can't believe I'm here. *How did I get here?*

In the bathroom, I open the mirrored medicine cabinet. There's Neosporin and calamine lotion. Pepto-Bismol tablets. A bottle of Advil and a bottle of hydrogen peroxide. The top shelf is stacked with boxes of bandages and a roll of medical tape. I think of my mom. What would my mom do back when she was being a mom? *Cold water.* It comes to me. The press of a cold washcloth on my neck when I tried Lauren's new curling iron.

I pull a washcloth off the towel rack and turn on the faucet. It's not ice cold, but I wet the cloth and wring it out. Then I grab another towel, the Neosporin, a box of gauze bandages, and the roll of tape.

When I walk back, Dillon is sitting against the pillows watching me. His arm is resting on his leg, the burned skin an ugly pinkish red.

"I'm sorry." He sounds tired. I can't look at him. I sit beside him and he shifts to give me more room. I lay the cool cloth over the burns. I press it down carefully. "Does that hurt?"

He shakes his head.

For a long time, we stay like that. Me pressing the cloth to his wrist even after the coolness of it has faded into the heat of his skin.

"Remember when I did this for you?" he says. "That first day at the pool?"

A tear leaks from the corner of my eye. I pull back the washcloth and pat his arm dry with the extra towel. The wax has hardened and most of it's peeled off. I don't know what to do about the bit that's sticking to his skin. I don't do anything. I squeeze Neosporin along the blisters and lay gauze over the top, two pads overlapping to cover all of it. Carefully, I tear strips of tape and smooth them over his skin and the edge of the gauze. When I'm done, I sit back, away from him, numb.

He shifts to his knees and then slides onto his stomach, crawling toward me, his body curling until his head is in my lap. I want to be angry. I want to push him away. But I also want to stroke his hair and whisper that it will be all right.

Because of course I remember.

"Maybe I can ask Mrs. Lyght about a deferral," I say. The words tug out of me from some deep place.

He turns so that he's looking up at me. "A deferral?"

"See if there's any way I could go next year."

"That would be . . . perfect. Next year would be perfect." His smile nearly breaks my heart. "You'll ask?"

I nod.

"I love you, Emma."

"I love you, too."

His breathing deepens. His hands are folded up by his chest but as he relaxes against me, his left arm falls open. The gauze is white against his skin, but I can still picture what's beneath. A line of red running down his wrist. As if he's slashed his vein.

"You and I," he murmurs. "We save each other."

19

It's just after midnight. I want to be asleep—so badly. Instead, I'm staring up at a ceiling I can't really see in the dark. There's something awful about lying awake in the dark.

In Pompeii, on its last day, the ash rose so high that it blacked out the sun. Everything, everywhere, was dark. I think of my fresco girl. Anna. How frightening it must have been. The not knowing. The panic when you can't see what's right there in front of you. The irony strikes me but it's not very funny. Here I am thousands of years later. I have a light by my bed. I can turn it on, but I'll still be in the dark.

I reach for my phone and when the screen lights up, I see a text from Mom. Great.

> Saw that WICKED is coming to Gammage next fall
> and thought of you. Maybe we can go together?
> Not trying to be pushy, by the way. Just miss you.

As if it's some kind of Pavlovian response, my eyes fill with tears. I miss my mom. The one who took me to shows, the one I could talk to about anything. The mom I have now, the one living with Henry . . . I have nothing to say to her. I haven't talked to her since my blowup at the house, but I promised Dad I'd go over for her birthday next week. It's amazing how he can worry about her when she doesn't think twice about him. I read the text again. I don't know how to reply so I don't. I clear the screen and pause.

It's too late to call Marissa now. Guilt climbs my throat as I struggle to swallow. I never called her back this week—I haven't even told her about Rome. How can I tell her what's happening now? Instead I dial Lauren. It rings twice and then I hear a tired "Hey."

Thank God.

"Hey," I say.

"Everything okay?" I can hear the wariness in her voice.

I hate that she has to ask. I hate that we've become the kind of family where things are usually not okay. I hate that things are absolutely not okay right now and I have no idea how to tell her that.

"I just wanted to call."

"You sound tired."

"So do you."

Her breath whooshes over the line. "I've got a huge paper due."

"It's Friday night."

"The paper is due Monday and tomorrow is Law Day at the Tucson mall. I'm volunteering from nine to five, don't ask me why." I hear a pencil hit the desk. "How's your project coming for the internship?"

"Oh. Um . . ."

"That doesn't sound good."

"No, I was just thinking about it and Pompeii." *And I was. Sort of.*

"You and disasters. Speaking of which," she adds, "did you tell Dad?"

When I'm quiet, she says, "Em. He's making her a birthday present."

"I know. I'm going to tell him."

I hear the frustration in her sigh. "Just let me do it."

"I'm the one who lives with him, Lauren. You agreed."

"That was a stupid agreement," she gripes, but I know that she'll hold to it. "So how is Mr. Perfect?" she asks.

"Don't call him that."

There's quiet on the line. "Em?"

He dripped wax on his arm.

I hear the words in my head but how can I say them? Once I do, I can never unsay them. And Lauren can never unhear them. Two years ago, when Marissa was dating Andy Tamura, they had a huge fight. She was hurt and sad and then so angry she told me he was an ass. *He picks his nose and then wipes his snot under his chair. I saw it.*

Four days later, they made up, enough to be friends again, but all I could think of whenever I saw Andy was him depositing his snot under chairs. And this . . . this is so much worse than snot. If I tell Lauren now, she'll never forget. Even when Dillon and I have forgotten, she won't.

Will I forget?

I squeeze my eyes shut and force a smile. "He's great," I say. "He brought me my favorite donut on Tuesday." I wince. That sounds so stupid.

"I'll alert the media," she says with a yawn.

"I should let you go."

"You sure everything is good?"

And I can tell by her voice that her mind has already drifted back to her books.

"Yeah, great. Night, Lauren."

"Night, Emmie."

I click the phone off and lie back down on my bed. He did bring me a donut, I tell myself. He brought me into his group of friends and made me feel like I belonged. He helped me mop up the mess called my dad without ever saying a word. When I skipped school after an obligatory weekend with Mom and her new family, he found me at the park. When I lashed out, he didn't run. When I wanted to fall apart, he wouldn't let me. He saved me, over and over, by loving me more than I thought anyone ever would.

And my first day at the community center, he saved my life.

20

I probably wouldn't have died that morning, but facial dis-figurement was a real possibility.

It was exactly eight days after I officially moved into the house with Dad. I'd had a teary goodbye with Marissa and come close to begging Lauren not to go back to Tucson but to transfer to ASU, closer to me. I'd boxed up all my clothes and my books and my treasures, and on the morning I left, Mom insisted on helping me load everything in the car. I stood there while she hugged me and managed not to cry until I was on the road. Cleo was in her carrier on the seat beside me and she cried with me for the entire hour it took to drive.

The only good thing I had to look forward to was my job at the community swim center. I'd brought up the topic of summer jobs one Saturday at Cupz and Dillon had told me he might be able to help me find one. The community center where he and Jace worked as lifeguards was always looking for help when summer programs began and kids flocked there to swim, hang out in the game room, and watch movies. He told me to call the center and ask for a woman named Susan Felix. When I called, all I did was mention Dillon's name and I had an interview.

Susan spent fifteen minutes with me, long enough to determine that I wasn't a felon, to look at my report card (all As), and to read a reference letter from the guidance counselor at my high school. She slid some papers in front of me, told me to fill them out, and the job was mine.

When I showed up for work at eight o'clock my first morning, Susan walked me to the concession booth and handed me a blue-and-white-striped shirt from under the counter. I buttoned it over the sleeveless eyelet blouse I'd worn with a gray cotton skirt.

She frowned at the pair of canvas Toms on my feet. "Those might get ruined. After the lunch rush, the floor in here will be a sticky mess."

"It's okay," I said. "They're old."

She showed me the drink cooler, the rolling grill for the hot dogs, and the variety of chips, as well as how the register worked. Cash only. I'd just had a lesson in how to operate the slushy machine when the phone on her belt started ringing.

"Now what?" she said in way of answering. She sighed and then gave me an apologetic look. "I'm sorry, Emma. I need to take care of this. While I'm gone, would you make up some more slushy mix? The containers and syrups are up there." She pointed to two wood shelves mounted above the machine. The lower shelf was stacked with bottles of syrup and Tupperware pitchers. "Cherry is always the most popular," she added. "I'll be back before the rush to make sure you have the hang of it."

She didn't come back.

The slushy machine had three compartments and they were already churning with cherry, grape, and bubble gum. I made up an extra pitcher of grape and bubble gum. Cherry was the problem. There wasn't any more syrup on the shelf above the machine. Instead, I could see the edge of a new bottle on the highest shelf, wedged in beside large square boxes. Napkins and paper cups, I supposed. A quick look at my watch showed I was running out of time. Tiptoes didn't work, so I tried jumping. I bumped the underside of the shelf and the bottle wobbled a little. If I could just hit it a little harder . . . Jumping again, I pushed at the *wood*, but instead of the bottle wobbling, the shelf did.

"Emma—don't!" I recognized Dillon's voice as the back corner caved and the weight of the boxes slowly tipped everything forward. Toward my head.

I threw up my arms but before I could get crushed, two arms were beside mine and Dillon shouldered me out of the way. "I got it," he said.

My head spun as I stepped back to the far counter. Dillon held up the shelf, his arms spreading to balance the weight, one leg forward, his head dipped between clenched shoulder muscles. It was like Atlas holding the world—if Atlas had been wearing a stretchy white swim shirt and blue swim trunks.

"The hook must have come out of the wall," Dillon said. "I'll tilt the shelf a little and see if you can bring down the boxes, one at a time."

Nodding, not that he could see me, I positioned myself by his side. The end box was big and unwieldy but not heavy. I grabbed it and let it drop lightly on the ground. Then I got a hand on the bottle of cherry syrup and the last box came down on top of the other one while Dillon lowered the wide wooden shelf, sliding it under the counter and out of the way. He let out a loud whoosh of breath as he straightened, chest heaving, hands low on his hips. "You okay?"

"Yeah. Fine."

He wiped a streak of dust from his forehead. "Welcome to the community center."

I smiled, laughing a little as some of my tension released. "It's going to be more exciting than I expected."

"Wait until you have thirty kids wanting hot dogs and slushies." He frowned and pointed to my hand. "Did you get that from the shelf?"

I looked down and only then realized I was bleeding. There was a scrape running from the edge of my pinky nearly all the way to my wrist bone. "I didn't even feel it."

His fingers slid around my right palm, and my breath caught. I already liked Dillon—more than I should have—but I also didn't want to read too much into his smiles. What if he was just being friendly? Dillon was Stupid Cute—the kind of boy who was so cute that you did stupid things around him. I'd fallen prey to Stupid Cute before. Like the time I carved "I love you" on a pencil and gave it to Robbie Thompson in the third grade. I didn't want to be stupid with Dillon. I was probably seeing something that wasn't there.

Feeling something that he didn't.

So I kept my eyes down, working to keep my breath steady.

He smelled like chlorine and coconut, and that seemed like a remarkably delicious combination—another reminder that I wasn't thinking clearly where Dillon Hobbs was concerned.

"I think there are bandages under the counter."

"Oh. I . . ."

"It's okay. I'm a trained professional." He pointed to the word LIFEGUARD stitched above his heart. "It's my job."

Three boys came racing up, barreling into the counter and grabbing hold with grubby fingers as they let their bodies swing like towheaded monkeys. "Cherry slushy!" one boy yelled.

"Me grape!"

"Sour drops!" the third said, all their orders overlapping, their legs banging the wood beneath the counter like a bass drum.

"Hold on," Dillon said. "Logan, get off the counter. All of you stop that banging." He fished some change out of his pocket and set it in front of them. "Go play a video game and then come back."

"But—"

"Now!" he ordered.

They grabbed the money, eyes wide, and took off down the hall.

Dillon shook his head and pulled a metal box from under the counter. When he opened it, I saw it was a first-aid kit.

"I can do that." I was embarrassed now.

"It'll only take a second."

He pulled out an antiseptic wipe and tore off the paper, letting the pieces fall to the counter. "So you all moved in to your dad's place?" His eyes flickered up to mine.

I nodded. "I'm trying to fix things up a little. Make it feel less like a rental house and more like us."

He smiled. "What's more like you?"

"Books. Old maps—I love old maps. Quilts."

"I don't get the whole quilt thing," he said. "My grandma makes them. Not comfortable."

I sucked in a breath at the coolness of the wipe against the scrape. "Yeah, but they're beautiful."

"But not practical for naps on the couch."

"You sound like my dad."

He looked up. "You're really close to him, huh?"

"He's a good guy." I watched him gently swab at the cut. "I'm glad I moved here, even if it does mean a new school my senior year."

"You'll like it at Ridgeway."

"Yeah?"

"We have block schedule, so that's pretty cool. Twice a week we have a food truck with decent pizza and rice bowls. Our principal likes to give inspiring speeches, but he has to take off his glasses to read, so he doesn't notice when everyone nods off. And," he adds, "you are friends with the captain of the baseball team."

"Captain?" I said, when really I was thinking, *Friends?*

"Just got voted in at the end of the season."

"Congrats. Are you guys any good?"

"We will be next year. You like to watch games?"

"I've never had any reason to before." I flushed when I realized how that sounded. If he was rolling his eyes, I couldn't tell—he was bent over my hand. Even the top of his head was beautiful, his black hair flickering with shades of purple and blue in the overhead light. He was too beautiful for me.

"Well, now you do," he said. He looked up. He was smiling and it was a flirty smile. I was nearly positive it was.

"Does it hurt?" he asked, nodding at my hand.

"It stings a little but not bad."

Now that it was clean of blood, I could see it was just a surface scratch, a little deep in the middle, but it didn't need first aid, not like this. Still, I didn't move, holding my hand out as if it would fall off without his attention. "I'm used to scratches from my cat."

"You have a cat? What's its name?"

"Cleopatra. She's very pretty but treacherous."

"Aren't all cats?"

"I take it you're not a cat person."

He shook his head as he reached for a Band-Aid. "Allergies."

"Oh." I could hear the disappointment in my voice and blushed.

"They're not bad, though. The allergies I mean."

Our eyes met. Held. *Definitely flirting!* My heart raced, rabbit-fast.

The sound of the Band-Aid wrapper crumpling startled us both. We looked down to see the bandage crushed in his hand. Red stained his neck as he tossed it out and grabbed another one from the box. He ripped the paper and peeled back the sticky tape and then laid it over the deepest part of the cut. He rubbed his thumb over it. Over my skin. My mouth dried up. My tongue suddenly felt five feet thick.

When my eyes rose, he was watching me. He smiled and I was suddenly, stupidly, happy.

"What's your last name?" he said. "I never even asked."

"Lorde," I said. "With an *e*."

"Emma Lorde." My name sounded special coming from his mouth, shaped by those lips, by his white teeth, by his breath that smelled like lemonade. I wanted him to say it again.

He closed up the first-aid kit. "I should get back. I've used up most of my break."

"Oh," I said. "Sorry."

"Don't be." He stashed the kit and then faced me. "I'm not."

As he left, I ran my thumb over all the places where his fingers had touched my skin.

And I thought about the myth of the Red String.

After my shift ended, he came by wearing a yellow tank and black board shorts, sunglasses propped on his head. "I'll walk you home," he said.

"I have a car."

His gaze held mine. "So do I."

With my heart fluttering like a caged butterfly, we walked the three miles to my house. I kept waiting for awkward pauses or for him to say something to break the spell. But he never did. We talked about the community center and his job as a lifeguard and our senior year and his favorite classes and how I liked to play in the dirt, as he called it. We also talked about hard things. Hidden things. About bad days. About leaving and being left.

It was at least a hundred degrees and I was sweating through my shirt. I was pretty sure my shoulders were getting burned and the broiling pavement was eating through the soles of my cherry-slushy-stained Toms. I didn't care. I was never so sorry to see my house.

"That's it," I said, pointing to the single story with patchy grass in the front and blue curtains that I'd hung the day before.

We stood there for a long minute. "How are you going to get your car from the pool?" he asked.

I blinked, realizing I'd forgotten all about that.

"I'll walk you back to get it." His grin tilted up at one corner.

I laughed and all the misery of the past year and all the misery that was waiting inside my house vanished at the sound of it.

He reached for my hand and I let him. Our palms were both sweaty and it still felt absolutely perfect.

On the way back to the pool, I told him the story of the Red String.

Since nearly the beginning, I've felt certain that Dillon was for always. We'd talked about it . . . late at night when we could whisper dreams and make plans that our parents would have called naive but that were real to us. We'd marry after college. Dillon would get his CPA, and he had some money from his dad saved up. We'd live in the area—he couldn't leave his mom—and I would go to grad school and work as a teaching assistant.

And now?

Guilt is like a chisel, chipping away at my conscience. Is it me? Is he right? Am I being selfish about this? Do I somehow not love him enough? Not as much as he loves me? All he wants is for me to stick to the plans we've made. And they were good plans. Great plans.

We can still follow that plan.

I keep coming back to the same thing. It's an internship. It's nine and a half months. I can go and come back and nothing has to change. I'm not his dad. I'm not going to leave him. Shouldn't he be okay with this if he trusts me?

The questions spiral around my head.

Is it me?

Is it him?

How did it turn into *him* and *me* when for so long we've been an *us*?

Is it so wrong to want Rome and Dillon?

Maybe because Rome is on my mind, I think of Julius Caesar and one of the most famous betrayals in history. Brutus, his close friend and ally, shoving a knife in Caesar's belly. I'm sick at the thought. I could never hurt Dillon—but even my thoughts feel like a betrayal.

I love Dillon. I owe him so much.

But do I owe him Rome?

My mind spins around questions I have no answers to. Sometime during the night I fall asleep and then wake up, again and again, so that when I open my eyes to hazy sunlight it feels like I never really slept.

It's morning, and I still have no answers. If I can't outthink my questions, maybe I can outrun them.

21

The sky is a soft blue when I leave my house, the sun a bright light I wish I could switch to dim. My eyes hurt. My legs are stiff, my feet heavy as I hit the pavement in my running shoes and head for the park. Tim McGraw is pumping through my earbuds and I try and match my pace to the beat, will myself to sink in to the song. If I'm lucky, I can lose myself in the music and the rhythm of running. For just a little while, I need the sound track of my own life to fade to silence.

It's not working. I'm nearly to the park and I still feel like both of my feet are bags of cement. I'm ready to turn around when I see someone bent over at the trailhead. I don't have to guess—not once I get a look at the bright yellow running shoes with pink lightning bolts. Only Jace.

"Tell me you got those on clearance," I say as I jog up.

"Really?" He looks at his shoes. "I was trying to tone things down."

I smile and adjust the visor on my forehead, hoping to hide

the puffy slits of my eyes. "What are you doing up so early on a Saturday?"

"Couldn't sleep," he says.

I tuck my earbuds under the strap of my jog bra. "There's a lot of that going around."

Our eyes meet and his understanding feels like a warm shot of espresso.

"Want some company?" he asks.

I nod, realizing that, yeah, I do. "Slow, though?"

"You're always slow." His smile is so easy and so *uncomplicated* I have the urge to hug him. Instead, I smile back. "Lead the way."

He starts to the right, which is the way we usually go. It didn't take me long to figure out that seeing Dillon on the trails that morning last February was a fluke. Dillon doesn't like to run early—he has so much trouble falling asleep that it's better for him to run at night and sleep in as much as he can. But I'm glad Jace is like me—up early.

The dirt path, used by runners and bikers, cuts a wide strip between the desert on our right and the city park on our left. There are trails shooting off into the surrounding hills, but if we stay on the main path it's a four-mile loop back around to where we started.

For a few minutes we're quiet as we settle into our pace. I'm finally feeling better—the fresh air and sun are working their magic. I can focus on the trail, never needing to look beyond the next step—it's a relief. Our feet strike the dirt in a comfortable rhythm, and I don't know if it's me adjusting my pace or him adjusting his, but we're in sync as the path veers left. Traffic noises fade and are replaced by the low hoot of mourning doves that are always flitting from tree to tree in this part of the trail.

"So what's new with your scholarship?" I ask. "Have you figured out what you want to do?"

"If I had, I'd be sleeping right now," he says. "But it's not just about what we want, is it?"

I nod, thinking about Dillon. "No, it isn't."

"I was lying in bed last night trying to think of something I do just because I want to," Jace says. He pauses, his breath sighing in and out in pace with our slow jog. "Not because it's something I should do, or need to do, or because it's the smart thing to do."

"And?"

"I buy annoyingly bright footwear."

"That's all you've got?"

"It's depressing, isn't it? I found my first pair of neon yellow shoes on eBay in eighth grade. Now I wonder—was I already feeling trapped back then?"

"Trapped by what?"

He dances lightly across an uneven stair of boulders. "I don't know. Normalcy?" He shoots me a look. "It's a surprisingly difficult concept to live up to, as in, a *normal* National Merit Scholar would *normally* jump for joy at receiving the Bergen Scholarship."

"And you're not jumping?"

We both shift right and Jace crosses in front of me as a biker comes into sight. Air swirls around us as he speeds by and Jace waves off a faceful of dust as he settles beside me again. "My parents think it's irresponsible for me to even consider giving it up."

My breath quickens. "You told them?"

"Just that I'm having second thoughts. Which have turned into constant thoughts."

I pull my eyes from the trail long enough to say, "Don't take it if you really don't want to."

He laughs, a short, sharp exhale. "You're the only one who's said that. Even Coach Diaz, who's also my guidance counselor, says to take the scholarship. He wants me to give it a year and then decide. Which makes sense. It's a reasonable compromise and it makes everyone else happy."

Again, I find myself nodding. I wish I didn't understand as well as I do.

Up ahead the trail splits into a V with a wide dirt path leading up and away.

This is how life works, too, I think. Paths splitting off in different directions. No markers to point the way. As we run past, I look up the slope. Just more brush and rock, but what happens when the trail crests the hill—what's beyond that? Part of me wants to hop over the rocks and uneven ground and follow that other trail. Screw the loop I know and the clock in my head that says I should get home and just . . . *go*. In the time it takes to draw in another full breath, the path has slipped farther behind and it's as if the trail doesn't even exist.

"So what about you?" he asks. "What do you want?"

"That's easy," I say. "I want to go to Rome and I want Dillon to be happy about it."

"He's not coming around?"

"You saw him at lunch the other day." The words swirl around us and disappear under our feet. If only it were as easy to leave my worries behind. Last night flashes through my mind. The sound of hot wax hitting his skin, the smell of cinnamon and the way the wax whitened and his skin reddened. I squeeze my eyes shut, wishing my mind were like a computer screen I could reset.

We're quiet except for our breathing as we climb the steep side of a wash and I find myself wanting to tell Jace—wondering if I can. He's Dillon's best friend; if anyone can help, it's him. I dig my legs into the hill and wait to clear the top before I say, "He's . . . acting weird . . . about it." My voice is a little ragged, but I can pretend the hill is responsible for that. "Have you noticed him . . . acting weird, I mean?"

"Weird how?" His breath is thready, too. "What's going on?"

I slow to a walk, my hands on my hips, my eyes on the trail, though I don't really see it. I can't do it. I can't bring myself to say the words—not even to Jace. "He didn't used to get so mad about things. Not like this."

"Yeah," he says. "He's been on . . . edge."

Something about the way he says the word makes my heart quicken. "Did something happen?"

"He got into it with Brian at practice last week." He gives me a quick look. "In Dillon's defense, Brian is an ass who regularly gets into it with everyone."

"But?"

"But Dillon always lets it slide—he has for four years."

"So what happened this time?"

"He lost it. Started yelling. Started shoving. Then Coach showed up."

"Something's going on. He's not himself, Jace."

"He's stressed like the rest of us. And Brian had it coming."

"I don't care about Brian."

He sighs. "I'll try and talk to him, but . . ."

"But what?"

His expression is pointed. Knowing. "It shouldn't matter if Dillon gets mad or not. You have to decide this internship for yourself."

I snort out a breath. "You mean the way you can't let your parents decide what *you* do?"

"It's totally different," he says. But his shrug concedes the point.

"It's hard, though, isn't it?" I say.

"What?"

"Giving up an opportunity that other people would kill for? It makes you feel stupid. Or crazy."

"Or both," he agrees. "But is that enough of a reason to say yes?"

"Fear of being wrong is pretty powerful."

"How can it be wrong if it's what you want?" He starts jogging again but flips around so he's running almost backward, which he knows drives me crazy. "Let me ask you a question."

"Don't do that."

"I'm not going to fall."

"That's what people say right before they fall."

He flips back around, his gait smooth and easy. For a lanky guy, six foot and still growing, he's got great balance. But if he goes down, he'll take me with him.

"What if you could do anything you want?" he asks.

"For the rest of my life, you mean?"

"Forget forever. Let's start small. Say . . . for the next ten minutes. What would you do? Not worrying about what anyone else thought or what you should do—just, what?"

I look up ahead at the open trail, the sun creeping higher and the blue of the sky that's so clear it looks like a never-ending sea. Suddenly, I have a lifting sensation like if I can just run fast enough I'll fly up into that sky. "I want to go back to the hill behind us and I want to run to the top, and then I want to sit there in the dirt and do absolutely nothing."

He stops, his brown hair a sweaty mess over his eyes, one dimple just visible in his left cheek. "Let's go."

22

"Jace—"

But he's already turned around and gestures for me to follow. As I stare at his back, something inside of me cracks
open and I want to laugh. But I can't. He's already at a sprint
and it takes everything I have to try and catch him. There's
no talking now as he turns up the trail we just passed and
though it's not a big hill, it's steep toward the top and I'm
panting and breathless when I pull up beside him.

He pushes waves of hair off his forehead and looks around.
He isn't as winded as I am, but at least his T-shirt is rising and
falling a little more quickly. "Nice."

It is. The air feels cleaner up here and there's no broken
glass or crushed cans. The hill is one of a series of rolling
hills and from here I can see the trail wind up and down
like a snake. The thought startles me and I look around my
feet.

"No snakes," he says, reading my mind. "Just a few ants

over there." He kicks loose some pebbles and flattens out a spot in the dirt for us, then sits. "Pretty safe right here."

My heart finally slowing, I sit beside him and glance at my watch.

"Not allowed," he says.

"It's been ten minutes."

"We'll get crazy and make it twenty."

So I rest my arms around my knees and let the sun warm my shoulders.

A few minutes pass and then Jace asks, "How's the research going?"

"I haven't gotten as much done as I wanted," I admit. "But I'm going to stay home today and really dig in. Pardon the pun."

"You archaeologists are such jokesters."

I smack him on the arm.

From the corner of my eye, I watch him fight back a smile. "So is your Pompeii idea going to work?"

"Believe it or not," I say, "I think it is. From what I can tell, the ring is made out of gold and with the snake motif, and the general design it fits the criteria of something from that part of the world, somewhere between the first and third centuries. So it could have been Anna's."

"Who is Anna?"

"That's what I call her." I explain about the fresco and how I've always wondered who the girl might have been.

He stares at me with a strange smile on his face.

"What?" I ask. I feel a blush and I'm not sure why.

"You're perfect for this," he says. "I'd love the research and figuring out where something came from and how it was made. But the way you're taking this ring and creating a life out of it—that's cool."

"Well." The temperature in my cheeks goes up a few more degrees. "I haven't done it yet." I pause to follow the fluffy white vapor trail of a small plane overhead. "So anything new on the coin? You said you had to check another source."

"Yeah, I meant to tell you. I was wrong about the back. It's not Faustina. It's Fortuna."

"Fortuna?" I rifle through my memory. "Roman goddess of good luck?"

"Not as exciting as a murdering adulteress, but they have very similar hairstyles."

"I'm sure they were often confused," I say. "What about the front of the coin?"

"It's got to be an emperor. The downside to a civilization that lasted five hundred years is that there are a lot of those."

"I'll get online today. See what I can find in the university's library."

"Check out the emperor Trajan. That's my best guess."

"Thanks." I stretch my arms to the sky. I'm already feeling the itch to get to work. To discover. To *uncover.* "This time next year I could be jogging through Rome," I say. I squint as a bit of sunlight flashes against something bright in the distance, creating a prism effect. Beyond the hills and the park, I can see neighborhoods of red tile roofs and the top of the school's stadium lights.

"If this were Rome, you'd be looking out at St. Peter's Basilica right now," Jace says.

I dig my hand in the sandy dirt, rubbing the grit between my fingers. "Supposedly it's like a lasagna."

"What is?"

"Rome. When you dig down, every layer is a different time period. There's a church, the Basilica of San Clemente, where the main floor was built in the eleventh century and you can descend one flight of stairs and be in the fourth century and descend a second flight of stairs and be in the second century."

"I want to see pictures of that."

"I want to *take* pictures of that."

Our eyes meet and we both smile.

"You have to go, Emma. This is too perfect for you."

"I want to."

"But?"

"But the competition is going to be tough. And there's Dillon. I don't feel right leaving him unless he's okay with it."

"It's just an internship."

"Hey," I say. "That's my line."

He meets my grin with one of his own and we go back to looking out at the view. The sun has moved higher in the sky, but I don't want to go. Not yet. Up here I don't have to think about melted wax or dented cars. Except that it's hard not to. "I thought about asking Mrs. Lyght if I could get a deferral," I say.

"What does that mean?"

"See if Dr. Abella might let me go next year."

"Why would he do that?"

"If I turn in a really great application, he might." But doubts nibble at me. Next year, Dr. Abella will have time to choose from grad students. Why hold the spot for me?

Jace turns away.

"You don't like the idea?"

"It sounds a lot like Diaz's plan for me to take the scholarship for a year."

"Well." I shrug. "Compromise is good, right?"

"And what if there is no next year?" he asks. "What if you stay here and I go to college and we all contract an antibiotic-resistant strain of infection and we're dead in a year?"

I roll my eyes at the question. "We wouldn't all die," I say. "Even resistant bacteria doesn't kill everyone."

"Conjecture."

"Historical fact. Spanish flu epidemic of 1918, Black Death in the Middle Ages, even smallpox. People always survive."

"History only exists where it can be recorded," he argues. "You're forgetting about the societies that were completely wiped out by disease."

"Which societies?"

"The ones we don't know about because no one survived."

I groan. "You're going to turn down the Bergen Scholarship and skip college because of societies that may or may not have existed in centuries past?"

"No," he says. The teasing note in his voice is gone and he sounds tired. "I'll probably take the damn scholarship and finish first in my class and then die of toxins consumed from plastics in our landfills polluting our water sources." He turns to look at me, his eyes serious. "That's why you can't defer. Why you have to go to Rome. It's my dying wish."

I muster a smile, wishing it were easier—for both of us. "We'll see. I haven't even asked Mrs. Lyght about the deferral. I figured I'd go in early Monday morning. I have to ask her about how to format my catalog entries anyway."

"About that," he says. "I saw it on the assignment sheet and was wondering if you wanted to look at my coin catalogs. Maybe steal ideas from how it's done? I could bring them in on Monday and you could get Mrs. Lyght's opinion, too."

"That's a great idea. You wouldn't mind?"

He pushes himself to his feet and reaches down a hand. I slip my dusty palm in his and let him pull me up. "For you, Emma, anything."

"Anything?" I tease as I brush dirt from my butt. "Wear plain white sneakers?"

"Let's not get crazy."

I laugh and adjust my visor against the sun. Then we head back down the hill.

23

When I turn the corner onto my street, my feet slow. Dillon's truck is parked in front of my house. He's leaning against the front grill, wearing the blue Henley I bought him because it matched his eyes. I remember the night I gave it to him and he pulled it on without undoing the buttons and it got stuck on his head. Laughing at him, I slid open each button from the bottom and kissed the bit of face revealed—his jaw, his bottom lip, the underside of his nose. It's always been such a good memory, but now it's shaded by what happened last night. Burning wax is part of our history now, and I don't know how to handle that.

The shirt has long sleeves, so his wrist is covered. If the burn is still bandaged, I can't see. Will it leave a scar? Will it be there as a daily reminder?

Why is it that the things you want to forget are the things you never will?

"Where were you?" he asks.

"Running." I slow to a walk and stop a few paces in front of him. Is he wearing the Henley because I bought it—or because of the long sleeves? I pull off my visor and fluff my fingers through my sweaty bangs.

"I've been waiting awhile."

He gives me his teasing smile, the one that shows the chip in his side tooth and always makes him look impossibly sexy. But my heart doesn't somersault. My stomach doesn't turn warm and liquid. Instead, I'm mad. How dare he look so rested—seem so happy?

"I didn't know you were coming over," I say. "I bumped into Jace. We ran the loop together."

He frowns as he looks down at my legs. "Did you fall? Your legs are streaked with dirt."

I shake my head. "What are you doing up so early on a Saturday?"

"I finally slept a little last night." He reaches down and I notice a plastic cup resting on the bumper. "I brought you a strawberry Frap. It's probably melted by now."

"Melted is still good. Thanks." The cup is almost a shock it's so cold and wet in my sweaty hand. I pull off the straw wrapper and take a long swallow. "Mmmm," I murmur. It is good—sweet and still icy. *Is this my Apology Frap?* I imagine myself asking.

He looks me over, his smile widening. "Let's go somewhere. Anywhere. Just you and me for the whole day. Your dad won't care, right?"

I take another sip and lick my lips. "I really shouldn't."

"Yeah, you should." He pushes himself straighter and

reaches out a hand toward my hair, but I step back and wave the drink in front of me.

"Dillon, no. I have to work on my application. I hardly got anything done all last week."

"You're going to get a deferral."

"I'm going to ask for one," I correct. I grip the cup in both hands and force myself to look straight into his eyes. "Was last night just a way to shock me into doing what you want?"

His surprise is genuine. "No! Emma, that's not it. This isn't a game to me and I know it's not a game to you. But you chose, don't you see? By asking for a deferral, you told me that I matter more to you than Rome." He pats his chest over his heart. "That's what matters."

"Then you can stop feeling insecure about us?"

"I know I've been an ass this week," he says. "But that's why I'm here. I want to make it up to you. Today is your day—anything you want."

I shake my head. "I can't today. In fact, I really need to work all weekend and I already promised to shop with Hannah for prom dresses. That'll take up most of tomorrow afternoon."

"But—"

"If I want to ask for a deferral," I say sharply, "it actually means I have to turn in an even more impressive application. Next year Dr. Abella will have way more options."

He reaches for my drink and sets it back on the bumper. Then he takes both my hands in his. My fingers are cold from the cup, and his feel almost feverishly warm. "Then just a few hours. Half of a day."

"I have a lot of research to do."

"I'll help you with it. Later." His eyelids lower. "Come on. I promise you'll have a good time. We haven't been together, just you and me, in so long. I miss you," he whispers. His lips part in a breathless smile. He slips his hands around my waist, tugging me closer.

I push at his shoulders. "Quit!"

He blinks. A dark flush colors his cheeks.

"I'm covered in sweat, okay? I just got back from a run." I wrap my arms over the bare skin of my stomach. "Give me a little space, please? Just until I get this assignment done."

His jaw squares and his eyes narrow. Exaggerating the motion, he takes one step back. "Is this enough space?" He steps back again. "How about this?" He backs around the side of the truck, yanks open the door, and climbs in. "Is this enough fucking space for you?" The engine fires to life and he revs the motor. Tears burn behind my eyes as I stumble up to the sidewalk. He drives off, my drink flying off the bumper. Strawberry Frappuccino is spread like an abstract painting across the asphalt. I bend to pick up the crushed cup.

Great. That went well.

Slowly I walk up the drive. I think I might start the morning with a bath and a really good cry.

24

"I feel like a giant blue cream puff."

Hannah comes out of the dressing room in a strapless blue dress with a poufy skirt layered in feathers and lace and glittering with sequins.

Normally, I'd be fighting off laughter, but nothing is normal anymore. Not even a shopping trip. "At least you won't have to worry about anyone else showing up to prom in the same dress."

Her lips twist in a wry Hannah-smile. I'm still mad at her about lunch the other day. I'm pretending not to be, but I'm too tired to give a very convincing performance.

Another girl moves off the platform and Hannah steps up beside me, the blue glittering from every angle in the wide expanse of mirrors set up at the back of the dressing room. We're not the only ones who are still looking for dresses on Sunday morning, two weeks before prom. The department store has a huge selection and it looks like half of them are back here. The racks are full of discarded gowns, and more hang over the dressing room doors. An exhausted-looking salesgirl, half buried in pink satin, is trying to clear dresses as fast as she can while girls come in with new armloads.

Hannah slips on a black stiletto that's lying in a pile on the platform.

"Now you look like a tall blue cream puff," I say.

"Why can't I find anything in blue that wasn't designed by a peacock?" She kicks off the shoe and turns her attention to my dress. "Oh, that one's beautiful, Emma. Total Cinderella."

I look at myself in the mirror, feeling a little like a princess. The sheath dress is made of apricot satin and hugs me from bust to hips and then flares around my knees. I shift to see myself from the back.

"Don't even think of asking about your ass or I'll have to shoot you." Hannah sighs. "I'd look like an asparagus in that dress."

I can't help smiling as I twist to make the fabric swirl around my legs. This is the fourth dress I've tried and it really is perfect. "I think this is the one."

"The color is great with your hair." Then her gaze shifts back to her own reflection. "Mine, on the other hand . . ."

"Why does it have to be blue?" I ask.

"Spence thinks retro is cool. But a vintage blue bow tie is way easier to find than a dress." Someone squeals near the front of the dressing room.

Hannah rolls her eyes. "Another happy customer."

"We'll find you one."

"I think I've exhausted my options here. I'm going to try the boutique that just opened by the gym."

We're barely off the platform before another group of girls takes our spot. Hannah leads the way to our dressing room and holds open the door for me. We're in a large corner room big enough for the two of us. As soon as we're inside, Hannah bends for the zipper under her arm. "So Spence said you guys are meeting us for pictures and then doing dinner on your own?"

"That's the plan," I say, focusing on my own zipper. Though Dillon hasn't said much about prom or anything. We're back in silent mode, but this time I'm glad. He needs to pull himself together and I need to finish this application. Once I do, I think things will be easier.

She pulls her dress down over a strapless bra and orange polka-dot thong. "I just wish Jace would find a date."

"I thought he didn't want to go?" I shimmy out of my dress, careful not to catch the fabric when I step free.

"If Lydia were still here, he'd go with her."

"As friends?"

"Or more. Who knows." Hannah snaps her shorts and straightens the hem of her yellow tank in the mirror. "You hardly knew her, but she was pretty great. Big heart. Always worried about everyone else first."

The words dig in to me exactly the way I'm sure she wants them to. Tired, I let out a loud breath. "And I don't, is that it?"

"I didn't say that."

"But you meant it." I hang the dress carefully, not wanting to take out my frustration on the delicate fabric. I'm pretty good at avoiding conflict, and part of me knows that there's nothing to be gained by arguing with Hannah. But right now I don't really care. I tug on my black tee and turn to face her. "Why don't we just get it all out there. All the bullshit at lunch the other day, the little comments you've been making. You don't think I'm good enough for Dillon, and you never have."

She blinks, surprised, but then she puckers her lips and folds her arms across her chest. "It's not a question of whether you're good enough *for* him. It's whether you're good enough *to* him. Do you have any idea what this prom means to Dillon?"

"It means a lot to me, too." I flip my hair loose of the neckline, heat rising along with my pulse.

"He's already asked me ten different questions about things you might like," she says. "He's made lists—*lists!*"

Someone taps on our door. "You almost done in there?"

"No," Hannah snaps. "Go away."

"Jeez," the girl mutters.

She waits for the footsteps to fade and then says in a softer voice, "I can't believe you'd take this internship without even considering what it means to him."

"Yeah, you made that pretty clear the other day at lunch," I say. "But I have considered him—I am. He'll be fine with the separation if you don't try to sabotage things."

She gives me a funny look. "You tell him you're leaving for a *year* and you really want him to be fine with it?"

"Not *fine*," I say. "But he can miss me and still be supportive. This internship is a once-in-a-lifetime thing."

"And Dillon isn't?"

"Of course he is!"

"Well, it might not seem like that, is all I'm saying. To Dillon, I mean." She lifts a dress off the floor and pulls one of her flip-flops free.

"Or you," I counter. "It's not exactly a mystery how you feel. How you think Dillon should feel."

"I don't have to tell him how to feel."

"That's what you were doing at lunch."

"Oh, please," she says. She slaps at the trailing hems of more dresses, searching for her other shoe. "Everyone at that table knows Dillon doesn't do well with goodbyes."

"It's not goodbye when you're coming back."

"It's goodbye when you're putting an ocean between you." She drags the other shoe free of a discarded blue dress and slides them on. "I know that if I had a guy like Dillon, I'd think long and hard before I left."

"But you don't." The words are out before I can stop them.

Hannah's cheeks flush a purple-red but she doesn't lower her gaze. "He's my friend, Emma. One of my best friends, and I'm worried about him." She practically hisses the words at me. The din of the dressing room fades until it feels like just the two of us in this stupid square room—mirrors on two walls to reflect both of our flashing glares. "I know he seems strong, but he's not. You weren't here three years ago when his dad died. You don't know how it was. There's a lot"—her eyes dip down and then rise to lock on my gaze—"you don't know."

Anger burns in the back of my throat. I hate these hints that she knows him so much better than I do. That she's been there when I haven't. She wants me to ask, but I won't. I don't need her to tell me about the feelings of *my* boyfriend. And before I can stop myself, I say, "Are you in love with him, Hannah?" My jaw is so tight I can barely get the words out. "Because it sounds like maybe you are."

She looks away, her ponytail falling over her shoulder so I'm looking at the stiffness of her back, the tight muscles running down her arm. I see her shoulders lift with a breath and then she turns back to face me. Though her cheeks are still flushed, her gaze holds mine, unapologetic. "Yeah, I was . . . but it was a long time ago. And he's never felt the same way about me. Not even close." She draws in a ragged breath, and for once there's no drama. Just her expression, stark and vulnerable. "But he's still my friend. One of my best friends, and I care about him. I want him to be happy." She sighs. "And he is. With you. As happy as I've ever seen him, and if I give you a hard time, then that's why." Her voice turns fierce. "Because I don't want you to screw it up and break his heart."

Emotion clogs my throat. I feel unsteady with surprise—and embarrassed that I misjudged her.

"I want him to be happy, too," I choke out.

"Well, good," Hannah says. She rolls her eyes, a dramatic gesture that doesn't quite hide the shininess of tears. "Then I don't know why you're picking a fight."

A laugh hiccups from my still-tight throat. "You're a pain in the ass, you know that?"

"Thank you," she says.

There's another tap on the door. "You almost done in there?"

"No!" we both shout at the same time.

I smile and reach for the hanger of my dress. "Come on," I say. "I'll pay for this and then let's try the boutique."

"I thought you had research to do?"

"I do," I say. "But I can't let my friend show up to prom looking like something barfed up by the Cookie Monster."

25

"How's it coming?" Dad asks later that evening as he flips on the office lights.

I look up from his computer and then rub my eyes. *When did it get dark?* My head is swimming in facts about the ancient art of jewelry making. "Huh?"

"You get too close to the screen. You always have."

I yawn and swivel the desk chair to look out the shutters, angling them up a little as I crane my neck to see the sky. It'sdark, which means I've been working since I got back from shopping four hours ago. My stomach gurgles, checking in and confirming that, yes, it's past dinnertime. "I got a lot done," I tell him. "I've pulled together all the facts for the catalog entries. And I really like how the essay turned out."

"That's on the serpent ring?" Dad clears papers off the other chair and sits. Our fight the other night is forgotten, and he's more like his old self lately. I know it's because of the book that's resting on the corner of his desk. The memory book. The key to unlocking Mom's heart. He hasn't seen Mom since parents' weekend at U of A last September, but he's started hinting that maybe her birthday this coming Saturday might be a good time to see her again.

I still haven't told him that she's living with Henry. Lauren will kill me, but I'm not sure I want to. Dad is happy—why ruin that? And I think I've figured out a way to handle Mom's birthday without the two of them seeing each other. Eventually he'll find out the truth, but what good comes from telling him now? He'd just fall to pieces and I'd have to put him back together again. I don't think I can. Since Dillon stormed off yesterday, I'm having a hard enough time just dealing with my own love life.

"From what I've read," I say, "whoever owned the serpent ring must have been very rich and of the highest status. The filigree work and the detail in the serpent's head would have been very expensive."

Dad nods. "It would have likely been a woman's ring. Men's rings were most often functional—signet rings that displayed the seals of their families."

"Dad!" I lean forward.

"What?"

"Don't help me!"

He grins. "Can I at least help with your application for the university?"

"It's all done. I submitted the online app and sent in all the test scores they requested. I'm just waiting to find out what happens with the internship before I send in the essays and letters of recommendation."

"Well, you don't leave much for your dad to do. At least I can feed you."

My stomach rumbles again, and now I can smell the onion and garlic. "Mmm, you made pasta?"

"With mushroom sauce."

"Let me finish this up."

He nods, and though I expect him to leave, he doesn't. He reaches for the memory book and pulls it onto his lap. "So have you spoken with your mom lately?"

"Dad." I angle my head toward the screen so my hair covers my face. "Can we not do this?"

"Her birthday is in less than a week. Plus, your prom is coming up. I know she'd like to be here for all the girl stuff."

I click save on my research and close the screen. "She's the one who chose where she wants to be—and it wasn't with us." I say it gently, but once the words are out, I find myself waiting, hoping.

"Choice isn't always that simple," he says. "We make choices not because of what we want but because of what we think we need."

I nod, though I have absolutely no idea what he's talking about.

He smooths a hand over the cover of the album. "I've been thinking more about it, and I'd like to go on Saturday and give this to her myself."

I close *Bodies from the Ash* a little more forcefully than I mean to. "We already talked about this, Dad. I said I would go." The last thing I want to do is spend the day with Mom, but if I go, then Dad won't insist on going himself. "You know it's better if I bring her the book. She'll be weird if you're there."

"But once she sees this . . ." He smiles. "How can she look through this and not open her heart to me again?"

He thumbs through the pages. I've always hurt for him— for the way Mom treated him. He's been the victim in all of this, and I never understood how she could turn away when he wanted to work things out—when he was willing to do anything to keep our family together.

But now, for the first time, I look at him with his needy eyes and his mouth hanging open and the nervous flutter of his fingers on the page . . . and I think of Mom. This book means everything to him, but how will it make her feel? Guilty? Trapped?

My phone chimes. Startled, I look for it.

"Dillon?" Dad asks as he closes the book. The name drips with disapproval. It has ever since the night Dillon slammed an elbow into his truck. Dad's never come out and said he saw what happened, but he knows something isn't right.

I lift some papers and check behind the computer monitor. "This isn't easy for him," I say.

"Is it easy for you?"

I sigh because Dad isn't going to understand no matter what I say. The phone chimes again and I spot the blue-swirl cover against the gray carpet. It's good that Dillon is texting. Maybe it was the talk with Hannah or maybe it's just the break this weekend and the fact that I've gotten a lot done on my project. I'm eager to make up with him and shift the focus back to prom. There's still a huge chance I won't get the internship and next year will happen exactly as Dillon and I planned.

But when I flip the phone to see the screen, the text isn't from Dillon.

"It's Jace," I tell Dad. "He's helping me with my catalog entries."

"I can help you with that."

"I know your kind of help. You'll tell me to do it the way you do it and Dr. Abella will think my famous father did the work. Then someone else gets the internship."

I haven't told Dad about the idea of deferment yet. So many things I'm not saying to so many people. Dad. Lauren. Marissa. *Crap!* I still haven't called her back. *Tonight—I'll call tonight.*

"It's fine to get a little help," he says. "You're only a high school senior. You can't be expected to know all of this."

"Which is why I'm going to get help—from Mrs. Lyght." I quickly text a reply and hit send. "Jace is going to meet me there in the morning. He's got a coin catalog I want to ask her about." *And deferment. Though . . .* I'm hesitating about it now. Does it make sense to bring it up tomorrow? Wouldn't I be in a stronger position once Dr. Abella has seen my completed application? Assuming I do an amazing job and he's impressed. Which is my plan.

Something snaps. I turn toward the window. "Did you hear that?"

Dad shrugs. "A wild rabbit, maybe? The cat from next door?"

I slide closer to the shutters. It's completely dark outside

174

now and I can't see much except plants outlined in the landscape lights. Still, a shiver of unease runs down my spine. I
reach for the rod that controls the angle of the wooden slats
and snap them shut all the way. Then I turn back to Dad.
"Let's have dinner."

26

I startle awake. My body jackknifes to a sitting position before I know what I'm doing. My heart is racing. *Why?* It's dark in my room—a thick black soup my eyes can't see through.

My breath catches, cold in my throat, while I listen. *For what?* I don't know what woke me. I strain against the darkness. A tiny click sounds to my left and I look down. The clock. The numbers have flipped to 2:00.

That's it—no other sound. My eyes adjust enough that I can see the room is empty. My heart slows and my breath quiets. I wish I had my cat, Cleo, now. I wish it was her jumping on my bed that had woken me. Her warmth settling beside me.

It must have been a dream.

I force myself to lie back, though I can't remember what I was dreaming about. I glance at the clock again, and that's when I see it. At first it's just a shape—something there that shouldn't be. Then the shape comes into focus—a dark curve resting on a small square sheet of paper. A dark curve with a bow. My heart trips over itself as I flip on the small lamp. A circle of yellow glows over the nightstand.

It's hair. A short, thick piece of hair tied in a red velvet ribbon. It's Dillon's hair.

Oh God.

And mine!

Jerkily, I drop it, my fingers like sticks. My eyes shoot to the window. The shutters are closed—or are they? Are they closed but not latched?

My fingers are shaky as I weave them through my hair. *My cut hair.* He was here. In my room.

He cut my hair while I was sleeping.

I fold my knees to my chest and wrap my arms tight around them. He means this to be romantic. A grand gesture. That's what this is. We watched a movie once, one of those old black-and-whites that we found flipping through the channels late at night. The woman gave a lock of her hair to her lover and he carried it with him in a book. I remember telling Dillon, "How romantic."

But this?

Panic beats inside my chest. Acid fills my throat.

He loves me. I know he loves me. *Oh God, how can love make my skin crawl?*

I open the tiny drawer in my nightstand and sweep the hair inside. *Away.* As the paper flutters, I see that it's a note with four words written in red marker.

I'd die for you.

27

"Well, if it isn't two of my favorite students." Mrs. Lyght smiles at us as she rocks back in her desk chair.

"You're only saying that because we brought you coffee," Jace says. He holds up the Styrofoam cup.

She straightens. "That's for me?"

The bribe was all his idea, but when Mrs. Lyght's smile turns into a surprised grin, I nod as if I ground the beans myself. Not that the coffee is still hot.

Jace was waiting by the flagpole when I drove up, ten minutes late. The parking lot was mostly empty, though there was a steady stream of moms in SUVs dropping off kids by the front gate. I nearly ran down one of them cutting through a spot. Jace watched me jog over, his head bent against the sun, one hand shading his eyes. When he kept staring even after I reached him, I flushed, wondering if my worries were clear on my face—or if it was just the puffy eyes from my sleepless night.

"What?" I snapped, more defensively than I meant.

"Just . . . catch your breath," he said. "We've got twenty minutes before the first warning bell rings."

What a stupid expression . . . *catch your breath.* As if it had run off somewhere. As if it were playing hide-and-seek. As if it weren't trapped inside the little drawer of my bedside table along with a ribbon of hair.

"You have no idea how much I need a decent cup of coffee this morning," Mrs. Lyght is saying. "Mondays," she adds, staring at the clutter on her desk.

There are piles of papers, and I'm guessing one of them is my quiz on turning points of the Civil War. As distracted as I've been these past weeks, I don't think I'm going to want that one back.

She takes the cup from Jace and gestures for him to pull up another chair. "I got Emma's email about having some questions, but she didn't say you'd be here, too."

"I've been helping a little with the research."

"I hope that's okay," I say nervously.

"Of course." She smiles softly at Jace. "I think it's a very nice thing."

Her voice rings odd to me—the words, maybe. Or the tone. But Jace is already shrugging that off as he pulls out his coin catalog and sets it on the desk facing Mrs. Lyght.

She takes a sip of coffee and runs her hand over the cover. "Did you go out and buy this?" She looks from Jace to me.

"No, I've had it for years."

"A catalog of ancient coins?"

"It's a pirate thing," Jace says.

"Don't ask," I add, and Mrs. Lyght laughs.

He opens the book to the page he's marked and I ask Mrs. Lyght about the similarity in the coins. "I think it's Fortuna," I say, "but the back is so worn down that I don't have enough evidence to be certain."

She adjusts her glasses as she studies the entry. "It happens all the time," she says. "Rarely is there complete certainty. Just present your evidence and your best guess based on the available information."

We spend another five minutes talking about how to format my catalog entries, and then the warning bell rings. My head is crammed with all the new information, but my heart feels a million pounds lighter. I can have the whole thing finished before the start of today's baseball game.

"Anything else?" she asks as we gather our packs.

The deferral. For the past few minutes, my stomach felt like an actual stomach and not a blender. But now . . . I sigh. Jace looks at me, his eyebrows raised enough for me to sense his own tension over this.

"Um." I swallow. "Not right now."

"All right, then," she says. "I'll look forward to getting the completed application by next Monday."

Something shifts at the door—a flash of something. A shadow. I catch it out of the corner of my eye but when I turn to look, no one is there. "Did you see something?"

Jace leans forward, angling his head toward the door, then shrugs. "No."

My shoulders are stiff, my hand gripping tight to my backpack when we walk out. I pause in the hall and take in a breath through my nose.

"What?" Jace asks.

"Nothing," I say. But it smells like Dillon's body spray out here. Except, it can't be—he never gets to school early.

"I'd better get to my locker," I say, giving Jace a wave as I walk off.

It can't be.

But I know that it is.

"He's trying to kill it."

Hannah leans forward, her fingers gripped around the bleachers just as tightly as mine. Dillon is up to bat but instead of his usual calm control, the bat is vibrating in his hand as if he wants to club someone in the head with it.

Today's game is away, against the Central High Lions. If we win, we'll clinch a spot in the play-offs, which start at the beginning of May. Hannah and I are on the top row of the bleachers as usual. Dillon's mom is on the bottom, and the other families are spread between us, most with little coolers and umbrellas against the heat that's steadily been climbing since last week. Dillon struck out his first time up, swinging out of his shoes on three straight pitches. And it looks like he's doing it again.

"It's all right, Dillon!" Hannah calls.

I almost laugh. As if anything is all right.

Dillon takes a huge cut at the ball. "Strike two," the

umpire cries. The other team bangs on the fence around their dugout, trying to rattle him. Normally, Dillon doesn't rattle. Normally, Dillon doesn't drip hot wax on his arm or sneak into my room at night with a pair of scissors.

"What's got him so wound up?" Hannah mutters.

I shrug, but I know it's all the same things that have me so wound up. I met up with him at my locker after I left Mrs. Lyght's room. He was already on edge—tapping an angry beat with his fingers on the locker next to mine. "You got my present?" he asked.

Present? "Yeah." I busied myself by straightening books and notebooks on the narrow shelf. I could hardly look at him. He'd crept into my *bedroom*. Cut my hair while I slept. I felt . . . violated . . . no matter how he meant it. "We need to talk."

"Yeah," he mimicked. "We do."

Crack. His bat makes contact, but it's a slow ball chopped short to the first baseman, who runs for it, scoops it into his glove, and then plants himself in Dillon's path to make the tag. It's a routine out—I've seen it a million times. Dillon will jog into the tag, and without breaking stride he'll turn around and head to the dugout. That's baseball.

But now, his shoulders and head are forward and instead of slowing, he's running even harder down the baseline. The first baseman steadies himself and—

I close my eyes as they crash. Even up here, I hear the thud of bodies and the cries.

My eyes flash open. The Lions player is on the grass, curled in a ball. His hands are over his face and someone yells, "He's bleeding!"

Oh God. Dillon is also on the grass but he's sitting. He pulls off his batting helmet and stands. A trainer from the Lions' bench is already racing out and the two umpires are trying to hold back the Lions' coach. Mr. Diaz is in the mix and then the shouting starts. Dillon is in the middle of it, in the face of the Lions' coach.

"Dillon, no!" I call out. Which is pointless because he can't hear me with all the commotion. From the look on his face, I don't think he hears anything.

"What is he doing?" Hannah cries. "He'll get thrown out."

My heart is in my throat. From the corner of my eye, I see someone run out of our dugout. Jace! *Thank God—he'll know what to do.* Jace pushes his way in and gets a hand on Dillon's arm. Already he's turned Dillon away from the ref. I see him nod, imagine him talking in his easy voice. *"It's okay. Let it go."*

Dillon smacks his arm away.

Hannah gasps. Or maybe I do.

He shoves Jace in the chest. Shoves him so hard, so unexpectedly, Jace goes down in the dirt. With a cry I can hear, Dillon falls on him, arms windmilling as he throws punches. *Punches!*

I'm on my feet, horror and disbelief buzzing in my head like a swarm of killer bees.

Two of our players, Ty and Jordan, pull Dillon off. Coach Diaz is next to them. They circle Dillon while Jace gets up. He wipes at his mouth and looks at his hand. I see the same shock on his face that I feel.

"Where's the trainer?" someone yells.

It's all over a few minutes later but my heart is still pounding. I sink to the bench. *It's too much. I can't deal with this.*

Coach has walked Dillon back into the dugout where I can't see him. Jace has disappeared in there, too, along with the other guys. Mrs. Hobbs is off the bleachers but standing still as a statue behind the fence. It's obvious she doesn't know what to do, either. Someone comes up the dugout steps and I start to stand, but it's just Jordan, our next guy up to bat. They're going to continue playing? As if nothing happened? A guy runs out from the Lions—someone new to play first base.

"You should go down there," Hannah says.

"And do what?" I look at her. "They won't let me in."

"At least see how Dillon is."

"What about Jace? Don't you want to know how he is?"

She flushes. "Of course. But whatever's wrong with Jace will heal. With Dillon, I'm not so sure."

I swallow hard. My head is shaking as if I have no control over it. As if I'm a puppet and the string has been cut.

The Red String.

This has to stop. Tonight.

Dillon's truck is parked in the back of Chapel House, a small building next to the park that's rented out for school banquets, weddings, and things like that. It's painted white and has a pitched roof and arched windows, which is how it got its name. Tonight it's closed up. Security lights paint shadows across the striped lot, empty except for the truck. It's just past eight o'clock but it feels later than that.

It's a clear night. The moon is pumpkin orange and nearly full as I park beside Dillon. Even with eyes achy and red from crying, there's plenty of light to see the dark shape of him sitting in the truck bed. I try for a full breath as I open my car door. I can't even remember the last time I breathed easy. When I sat on the hill with Jace?

I shudder a little. Jace's bottom lip is split and swollen. His cheek is scraped raw just below his left eye. For the past few hours I've been at his house. It's the only place where I knew I'd feel a little less lost. Dillon left the game with his mother, who spared one second to tell me, "He'll call you later."

So I sat with Jace on his front step while he pressed a frozen bag of peas to his face. And, as generous as always, he'd tried to make me feel better.

"It's not your fault," he said. And, "Dillon will be okay."

"What about you?" I asked.

"This?" he said, moving the bag off his cheek. "This is nothing. Dillon and I have done worse to each other just messing around."

"This wasn't messing around."

The phone rang then, and I could hear his mom answer and bits of her half of the conversation. *He's fine . . . teenage phase. His father and I . . .*

Jace groaned. "They have everything figured out. Glad someone does."

After that, we sat there quietly as dusk crept in and swallowed up the day, one shadow at a time. I knew both of us were trying to see into the future. And I couldn't. I couldn't see myself . . . anywhere. That was what frightened me most of all.

That the present could wipe away the future.

"I think I'm going to break up with him."

I heard Jace draw in a sharp breath and closed my eyes. "Emma—"

"Don't say anything," I told him quickly. "I just needed to say the words. To see if I could."

He shifted beside me and I felt the tentative touch of his hand on my back. It was strange to fit myself against a different shoulder, awkward at first. But it was also Jace, the one person I knew I could lean against. We sat like that a long time, until the sky was an unbroken shadow and my phone finally beeped with a new text.

Dillon.

It was a relief. This couldn't go on—*I* couldn't go on. I'd never imagined that I could break up with him, but that's what I had to do. He needed to deal with whatever was making him act like this. It wouldn't be forever, I told myself. It would be more of a separation than a breakup. That's how I'd say it.

So here I am. Walking toward . . . what? I don't know what to expect. I don't know who I'll find. Which Dillon . . . the one I love or the one who has begun to scare me?

My heart races, my fingers fisted around my keys as I make my way over the cracked asphalt. I feel like I'm walking along a balance beam, nothing beneath me and no one to catch me. Like I need to be very careful. Bracing myself, I grab hold of the open tailgate and come around to where I can see him and he can see me.

He's sitting on a bed of blankets, his arms around his bent knees. His skin is sallow in the moonlight, but his eyes . . . it's him. It's the Dillon I fell in love with.

He smiles sadly. "I want to be strong for you, but I'm not, Em."

I climb into the truck and settle down beside him. My fear is swallowed in a thick layer of sorrow. His hair is stuck to his forehead and I lean in to brush it back. I smell his breath then—the sweet hoppy scent of beer. There's a small red cooler by his side and my stomach dips. Dillon doesn't drink. I didn't know he even had a way to get beer.

"How is Jace?" he asks. He tilts his face to look at me. "You were with him, weren't you?"

"I stopped by to see how he was. He's okay. He said it was nothing."

"He likes you, you know. He always has."

"Jace?" I shake my head. "He's a friend, Dillon. He's my friend because you're his best friend."

"Am I?" He leans back and stretches his legs out in front of him. He's in loose gray sweats and a Ridgeway tee. I'm still in my purple tee and jean shorts from today, along with a black sweater I found in the car. It's zipped to my neck but the cold I feel comes from deep down inside.

"Then why is he trying to break us up?" he asks.

"What are you talking about?"

"I saw him with you at school this morning."

The lingering smell in the hallway. "It *was* you," I say. "Why didn't you come in if you were there? Or were you spying on me?"

"I wanted to be there to support you. I knew it would be hard for you to ask for the deferral. I wanted to make it easier. But you didn't ask, did you?"

I flush with guilt. "It didn't make sense to ask today. First I need to finish the application, and if I impress Dr. Abella, I'll be able to make a request."

"I heard you talking about the assignment. Laughing. You and Jace."

"Is that why you jumped him today?"

"I was fighting for you, Em." His eyes flash up to meet mine. "I'll always fight for you. Whatever it takes." He reaches for another beer. There are new scrapes across his knuckles from today. Another reminder I don't want.

I shift away and something presses under my thigh. I reach down and from under a fold of the blanket I pull out something hard and flat. It's a brown leather sheath—a carved wooden handle jutting above a silver snap. I've seen it before on the shelf in the guesthouse with Dillon's dad's things.

I hold it up, the moonlight glinting off an edge of the sheathed blade. "Dillon," I say with a dry mouth. "What are you doing with your dad's knife?"

"We didn't do a lot of things together, my dad and I." Dillon takes the knife and slides it out of the sheath. The metal glints almost blue in the moonlight. "He didn't like sports the way I do. But he liked camping and fishing. We'd go once a year, just the two of us. He'd always bring this knife." He turns it so I can see the serrated edge of the blade, the sharp, curved point. "He loved this knife. I think he was always more sorry to leave it than me."

"Oh, Dillon," I murmur. "I'm sure he hated that he had to leave so often."

He shakes his head. "I think he was happy every time he walked out the front door."

The lump in my throat turns to ice. It's not what he's saying as much as the way he's saying it. His voice dead and cold, like the knife in his hands.

Dear God—the knife. Absently, he's twisting the tip into the pad of his thumb.

"Dillon," I manage in a choked voice. "Give me the knife, okay?"

"Maybe it's me," he says as if I haven't spoken. He raises his left palm and stares at it. The knife circles the air in his right. "Maybe I'm not made to be loved."

"Your dad loved you, Dillon."

"He could have stayed at home. Could've taken a desk job at the paper. But strangers' lives were always more interesting than mine."

I follow the movement of the knife. "Dillon." I reach for it, but he shifts his hand out of reach.

"What about your mom? You know your mom loves you. More than anything."

"I once had my palm read," he says, continuing as though he doesn't hear me. "Have you ever had your palm read?"

I shake my head. My gaze flickers back to the knife.

"My mom took me and Jace to the Renaissance Festival. We were in the fourth grade and we got it in our heads to dress up. Mom found us these shirts on eBay with padded shoulders meant to look like armor."

I nod and smile, forcing myself to stay calm, my eyes never leaving the knife.

"Mom bought us plastic swords and we had fights on a grassy hill and ate turkey legs and roasted corn. Then, on our way out, we passed the market and a woman in a long red dress and black hair to her waist asked if the young master, meaning me, would like his fortune told."

"And you said yes?"

"Jace thought she was weird, but I got Mom to pay and we

all went into her open tent. She had a table covered in velvet and strands of crystals hanging everywhere. She told me to sit down and then to show her my left hand." He holds it up and stretches his fingers wide. "She said she could read my future in the lines of my palm."

He looks at me, a half-smile on his face. "Like it's already all here, written on our hands. Do you think it is, Emma?"

"No, Dillon, I don't."

Using the knife like a pointer, he draws a line in the air above the base of his wrist to the vee between his thumb and pointer finger. "She told me this was my life line. She said mine curves and that means I'm a strong person. Full of energy and enthusiasm."

"Dillon, put away—"

"Then she wanted to tell me about my heart line." He points with the knife again. "It's this one at the top of your palm."

For a second, his lips tilt into a boyish smile. "I made a face and Jace busted up. My mom said that was enough, but I wanted to hear more. I didn't care about heart stuff, but I wanted to ask about baseball. The woman laughed at me. 'You'll change your mind one day,'" she said. Dillon frowns at the memory. "I think about that sometimes." His eyes shift back to my face and he studies me, the smile replaced by a look I can't decipher. "I wonder now if she would have told me about you."

"She would have come up with something that sounded good and meant nothing."

"You don't believe in palmistry?"

"As a way to tell our futures?" I shake my head.

"But it's old. You like old things."

"It was just a way for people to make sense of what they couldn't control. There's no truth to it, though. I mean, the Romans used to read the future in the chopped-up genitals of sheep."

I'm trying to be chatty, funny, anything to break his terrible mood, but instead it darkens. I silently curse myself for bringing up Rome.

"Jace says I should let you go. He says you'll hate me one day if I don't." His fingers squeeze around the handle of the knife. "Maybe you hate me now."

My muscles tighten as if I sense a shift of the ground beneath me. "Of course I don't hate you."

"I looked it up."

I blink, confused. "What?"

"The heart line." He stretches out his fingers again, shifting his hand until he captures enough moonlight to see the dark creases of each line. "Some people have lines that go all the way from their pinkies to their pointer fingers. I'll bet yours does, doesn't it?" He doesn't wait for an answer. "Mine cracks and trails off."

"It's just a line."

"It's shallow," he says. "You can barely see it." He runs the knife over the line again. "Maybe if my love line was deeper, you'd stay. You wouldn't want to go to Rome." He runs the knife over the line again; this time, a thin line of red trails from the edge of the knife. "Maybe my dad would've stuck around."

"Dillon!"

"I know why you're here and I don't blame you."

Fear pulses through me with every speeding heartbeat. "I'm here so we can talk. So we can work things out."

"You want to break up with me. I'd do anything for you and it's still not enough, is it? You still want to leave me."

"No—"

"But if I can make my heart line deeper, if I can show you how deep my love goes—" He slides the tip of the knife up the line and then down. Blood wells up, coats the edge of the blade, gurgles sickeningly as he saws at his own skin, almost robotically.

"Stop it!" I scream. I grab his wrist with both hands, but he doesn't quit. He drags my hand with his so I feel the press of the blade against his flesh.

I'm on my knees, all my strength focused on stopping him. I can hardly see through the blur of tears as I cry, "Stop! Stop! Stop!"

His hand shudders, trembles. The knife hovers just above, his strength too much for me. "I won't go," I cry. "I won't leave you . . . only, stop!"

"Do you love me, Emma?"

"Yes!" I scream. "I love you."

The muscles of his hand ease and I grab the knife. Blood is everywhere, all over his hand and his sweats and the knife and now my hand and my bare legs. The rusty wet scent of it makes my stomach heave. I lurch for the side of the truck and barely get my head over before vomit burns up my throat and spills to the pavement below. My whole body convulses and I let it all come up—I want it all out of me. Finally, nothing is left but gasps. Shakily I wipe my mouth on my sweater and collapse back in the truck. My face is wet with tears and snot, and my chest heaves for breath.

"It's okay," Dillon says in a comforting voice.

I burst into new sobs. He's watching me, concern in his eyes. *For me.*

His hand is an open wound. "Dillon," I say. I gesture to his hand. He stares at the blood almost curiously, as if he doesn't feel anything. *Is he in shock? Am I in shock?*

"We need to get you to a doctor. Let's call your mom and—"

"No."

"You're bleeding!" I dig around in the blankets beneath me, looking for something I can wrap around his hand. Then I remember. There's a thick headband in my purse. When I have it, I turn back to him. "Give me your hand," I say.

"You have blood on you," he says. "My blood."

"Give me your hand," I say again.

"Will you give me yours?"

"What?" I cry. I'm ready to shatter into a million pieces. I don't know what he's talking about.

He shifts to his knees so we're at the same height. He takes my hand and presses his palm against mine. The stickiness of his blood makes me want to vomit again.

"Blood vows," he says. "Remember?"

It takes a second—my mind is a whirl—but then it comes to me and I nod. I told him once about an ancient Wiccan ritual called blood binding. It was said to be a marriage ritual where a man and woman would draw blood from their fingers and drink it in a cup of wine. Then they'd join hands and be bound by words and by blood. Dillon laughed about it. Said Communion wine would be just fine for him.

"This is our blood vow," he says fiercely. "Nothing will come between us." His breath is fast and ragged as his eyes begin to burn with a different sort of heat.

"Dillon, please—"

He turns in one quick motion, his weight pushing me down in the bed of blankets. "I love you, Emma. Let me show you how much I love you."

"Your hand!"

His shape is above, blotting out the moonlight. His left hand is still pressed to mine while he uses his right to tug down his sweatpants and yank open my shorts.

No no no no no no no no no no.

I want to push him off me. I want to crawl out of my skin and run. But I'm trapped by his weight. Trapped by his tears on my cheek and the broken murmur of his voice whispering my name, over and over.

A desperate prayer. An aching plea.

He's not himself. He doesn't mean to.

I swallow a sob and let him take what he needs.

With my face turned into the blanket, I squeeze my right hand into his left and force pressure on the wound. I need to keep him alive—that's what matters. His blood is dripping down my arm and I have to keep him alive.

He needs help. I have to get him help.

When it's over, Dillon collapses, pressing his face to my shoulder.

"I'm sorry," he cries. "I'm so sorry."

"I know." I lift my face to the sky so I can breathe. "It's okay," I say. "Everything's going to be okay."

I wonder if anyone has ever spoken those words when they weren't a lie.

It is raining white.

The gray stone has long since spent itself on the roads and roofs of Pompeii and something much worse has been falling. The rock is larger and whitish like bits of bones, bleached in ash.

Anna is lucky to be alive.

As the world collapsed around them, Marcus pulled her, stumbling, down a narrow flight of stone steps and into a basement with scarred wooden walls and floors. One oil lantern provides a small golden glow on their huddled forms and on the stacks of goods that lie in broken piles at the opposite end of the storeroom.

Down here they are protected from the timber, plaster, and heavy ash that is raining down above them. But they are not safe.

They are trapped.

The remaining household slaves lucky enough to dodge death have also gathered here, each praying to his or her own god.

"We will be fine," Marcus says. He clutches the wooden chest. "The rock will stop and the dust will settle. We will be the lucky ones. The smart ones. Surely the gods have willed it."

"The gods have willed this?" Anna says in a voice that shakes like the earth.

"You will see," Marcus says. "My father will reward my bravery. He will buy your freedom."

Anna has never felt less free than she does now.

"Where is the ring I gave you?" Marcus asks.

Remembering, she unties the pouch and pulls out the ring. Even this day cannot completely dull the glimmer of gold. Squeezing her eyes shut in a quick prayer, she slides the ring over her finger as the night thickens around them. The rock rises higher and higher, the sound of it an agony that Anna dreams of escaping.

"We will be fine," Marcus repeats, over and over.

Anna rubs the ring and tells herself that she will live through this. The ring is proof—it must be. And so she waits, and hopes.

31

Dillon makes sure I get home safe.

He hums to the radio, one arm draped over the wheel, the other reaching every few minutes to touch my hair, my shoulder, my thigh. His left hand rests lightly on the steering wheel, the sterile tape a three-inch stripe of white that circles his hand and holds the thick gauze bandage in place.

"Are you okay?" he asks every few minutes. When we pull into my neighborhood, he slows the truck to a crawl. "You're so quiet. Don't be so quiet. Em. You're okay, right? We're going to be okay."

I nod.

"We've got prom in less than two weeks," he says. "It's going to be so special. I'm going to make sure it's special."

He talks and I let his words wash over me like the saline the nurse poured over his wound. Maybe I should have told her. My instincts said no—not with Dillon sitting there—but can I trust my instincts? I'm focused on what I need to do, but I'm also scared. Very scared. *I need to be careful. I need to do this right.*

We only waited fifteen minutes at urgent care before a pretty nurse with blond hair and pink lipstick cleaned out the wound and gave Dillon something to numb the pain and a tetanus shot in his shoulder. "You're very lucky," she said, watching as he tapped each finger to his thumb. "It doesn't look as if you've cut any tendons." Then the doctor came in and knit together the edges of Dillon's torn flesh with twelve stitches. Everything sewed up nice and neat. Dillon is eighteen, with his own insurance card, and at that time of night no one seemed interested in asking a lot of questions. An accident, he told LeAnn, the nurse. He'd been slicing an apple and the knife slipped, momentum forcing the knife across his hand before he realized. It's the same thing he'll tell his mother later.

I held Dillon's good hand and imagined following the nurse out to the hallway and pulling her into an empty room. *My boyfriend did that to himself,* I would tell her.

And then what?

Would she even believe me? Dillon had her charmed in thirty seconds, and he was so relaxed that I kept looking at the cut on his hand to remind myself that it was real. *I* was the one shaky and on edge.

"Can I get a drink for my girlfriend?" Dillon had asked. "Do you have Gatorade or something with electrolytes? Emma can't stand the sight of blood."

So LeAnn brought me a blue Gatorade and I drank it while she layered ointment and gauze pads over the new stitches, taped everything down, and instructed him to see his family doctor in twenty-four hours and have the dressing changed. Then she smiled and proclaimed Dillon good as new.

He turned and smiled at me. "I'm fine, Em. There's nothing to worry about. I promise. I'm fine."

And I could see in the deep blue of his eyes that he absolutely believed it.

When he pulls up in front of my house, he shifts the truck into park and gets out to jog around and open my door. I take his hand and step out into the cold. The stars are visible now, and I don't remember ever seeing a moon quite so pretty.

"I'll pick you up in the morning and we'll get your car," he says.

I shoulder my purse. "You sleep in," I say. "I'll go for a run and get it. It's not far." My car is still in the parking lot of Chapel House. He wouldn't hear of me driving home alone this late. Too dangerous.

"You sure you're okay?" His voice is soft and full of concern. Whatever drove him in the truck is gone. Bled out.

For now.

I wait with an ear to the front door until I hear Dillon's truck drive off. Then I lock it. Dad left the hall light on for me. I texted that I was staying at Dillon's to watch a movie and I'd be home around eleven. I set my purse on the kitchen island, then slip off my sandals and walk barefoot down the hall, through my bedroom and into the bathroom.

I raise the seat of the toilet and throw up blue Gatorade.

* * *

I was sick like this the night Mom admitted she'd been having an affair with Henry Ramos. Lauren reacted with questions and fury. I ran from the room and threw up. When my mind can't handle something, it's as if my body tries to get rid of it. If only it worked that easily.

My mouth feels bruised and burned with the taste of vomit. I turn on the shower. It only takes a second for the heat to build, for the spray to prickle hot against my hand as I test the temperature. I shed my clothes, shivering as they come off. I climb into the shower and close the sliding glass door.

The water stings my skin, so hot my flesh shrinks. I suck in air. I want the heat to cleanse me, to wipe the memory of this night off my skin. I reach for the soap, and when the water runs off my thighs in shades of rust, I look away. Tremors run through my body, spasms I can't control.

This is the kind of thing that happens to girls who skip class and hang out at the 7-Eleven with guys who get drunk in the afternoon. It's not supposed to happen to me. And Dillon—he's not *violent*. He never even loses his temper. I've teased him about it, how he gets quiet and contained. How he gets that measured voice that I hate.

But now I'm going over our history, shining this new light into the dark corners of my memory. There have been a few times lately when I've seen that anger build. The day the team lost a baseball game because he thought some of the guys were slacking. The night when the computer froze and he couldn't upload an economics paper that was 50 percent of our grade. Both times, he got mad enough that I saw cracks in his control. Nothing like this—just curses and clenched fists, rigid muscles that I couldn't relax. He said he was tired and went home early. But was it more than that?

And that morning in February. I came over on a Saturday, fresh muffins in a bag, and found shards of pottery sticking up from the carpet of the guesthouse. An accident, he explained, his eyes bleary with lack of sleep. He was drinking from a coffee mug on the treadmill and it flew out of his hands. But there was a stain of liquid on the wall—not by the treadmill but by the front door. I ignored it at the time, more worried about him than anything, but now I dissect the memory, wondering if it wasn't an accident at all.

I lean a hand against the tile and find my balance. *I have to face this.* Dillon isn't fine. He's a long way from fine. What if he hadn't stopped tonight? What if I couldn't make him stop?

I'd die for you.

I think of the note in my nightstand. I keep telling myself they're just words. People say them all the time. *I* say them all the time.

I'd die for another hour of sleep.

If I have to sit through another calculus lecture, I'll kill myself.

But tonight it was more than words. The memory of the knife and his hand and the blood . . . and what came after. I double over, my stomach heaving, though there's nothing left to come out.

I catch my breath, pressing my head into the corner of the

shower, feeling the spray sting my back. Dillon told me the details of his dad's death on one of our first dates. I wanted to hug him, but we were still new to each other. So I held his hand. I felt the strength in his fingers. I liked the clean, even cut of his nails, the rough calluses from playing baseball, and the warmth of his skin—the way it made me warm to touch him like that. Dillon told me it was hard, the way his dad left all the time, the way he had no control over when or how long. I knew it hurt him—we'd talked about it. How both of our parents had made choices that didn't include being with us. My mom had chosen another family. His dad had chosen a job.

How does a father leave his son?

How does a mother leave her family?

It's one of the connections that brought us together and the one that binds us so tightly. We've been hurt in the name of love—both of us have had our faith shaken. We promised each other that love would mean something different for us. Something real and lasting.

And now he needs help. I have to help him, but how? I scrub shampoo through my hair, the almond honey fragrant in the steam, and feel my head clear. There's someone who will know exactly what to do—*of course*. I close my eyes at the sense of relief. The water flows over me and I let it wash away my fear. Tomorrow I'll get us both the help we need.

I ring the doorbell and then step back, beyond the word WELCOME that's scrolled in gold across the shiny black mat. I'm not sure if it's ever really been extended to me. A small fountain gurgles just behind a bench covered in thick gray cushions and surrounded on both sides by wrought-iron candleholders with cream pillars. The home is painted the same neutral cream and fronted by carefully ordered desert landscaping. It's as neat and contained as Mrs. Hobbs.

The door opens and surprise registers on her face for a second, and then Mrs. Hobbs surprises me by . . . smiling.

"Emma. What brings you here?" She checks her watch. "It's only four o'clock. Dillon is still at practice."

"I know. I came to talk to you. Do you have a minute?"

"Of course. Is everything okay?" A flash of worry darkens her eyes. She's much lighter in coloring than Dillon—he obviously got his olive skin and black hair from his dad's side. But Mrs. Hobbs has the same beautiful blue eyes, though hers are usually cooler. She's never quite trusted me with her son, which I figured was just her being overprotective. Now I'm starting to understand why. She looks beyond me as if to be sure I'm not being followed—by who? Police? An ambulance? I suddenly wonder how she found out about Mr. Hobbs being killed. Was it a phone call? Was it a knock on her door like this?

"Everything is fine," I say. "I mean. Sort of." I flush. I always feel like such a teenager around Mrs. Hobbs, but for once I don't care. I'm glad she's a helicopter mom who always knows exactly what to do.

I follow the sweep of her hand as she gestures me to the living room. As many times as I've been to this house, I've never actually sat in this room. The couches and chairs, the carpet, even the drapes and paint are all a shade of pale beige. Even I'm beige today. I'm wearing a cream blouse over light khaki cropped pants. Gingerly, I sit on the edge of the couch and watch her sink into an armchair. Mrs. Hobbs runs a consulting business from home. I'm not sure what she does, but she's always dressed in nice blouses and pleated slacks. Sitting across from her now, I feel like I'm on an interview. I wish she'd suggested the kitchen. The kitchen is an easier place to talk.

"I'm glad you stopped by, Emma," she says.

"You are?"

"I owe you an apology."

I feel the pinch of my eyes as I frown. I wasn't ready for this and my mind is so sluggish I don't understand.

"I'm sure you know I've had concerns about your relationship with Dillon," she says. "In all fairness, I would have felt that way about any new love in his life." She crosses one leg over the other. "He's much more sensitive than most people realize, and the summer before he met you he'd had his heart broken by a girl that he cared for."

"Kiersten?"

"That's right. And then you came along and your relationship seemed to get very serious, very quickly. I couldn't help but worry, fairly or not." She purses her lips and draws in a breath that whistles through her nose. "Frankly, after these past couple of weeks, I was worried that it was happening all over again. But he told me this morning that you'd decided not to apply for the internship."

"He . . . he told you that?"

She smiles. "Well, it wasn't hard to guess. He was in such a wonderful mood." She leans forward to adjust the angle of a picture frame on the coffee table. There are three frames grouped at one corner—two of them are Dillon's school pictures and the third is a family portrait. "Of course, I was angry about his hand," she says. "Such a careless thing with the team making the play-offs. He's lucky Coach Diaz didn't bench him. As it is, he won't be able to do more than watch practice for a few days until our doctor gives the okay."

My eyes flicker back to the family portrait and Mr. Hobbs's small, unreadable eyes. For Dillon's sake, I hate him. I wish that Dillon could have hated him, too, and then he wouldn't have been so hurt. Why are we hardwired to love our parents? Why shouldn't they have to earn it like everyone else?

"The point I'm trying to make," she's saying, "is that I'm

no longer worried. What you've done for my son means so much." The fine lines around her eyes deepen with her smile. "You have no idea how happy you've made him. And me."

I swallow, my throat still raw from last night. I have to look away from the approval shining in her eyes. "Actually, that's what I'm here to talk about," I begin. "Dillon isn't . . . happy. He's not really okay."

Fabric rustles and she leans forward on the chair. "Did something happen today?"

"No," I admit. In fact, it was almost surreal. Dillon handled all the ribbing about his hand, laughed louder than anyone when Spence brought him an apple at lunch. It was as if he believed his own story. The only real tension came from Jace, and Dillon didn't seem to notice.

Jace. He looked awful—his bruises brighter against the unnatural paleness of his face. His lip still cracked and swollen, so it was painful to watch him try to eat. His text inviting me to run was waiting when I woke up, but I could barely get ready for school, much less manage a run. Instead, when I got to history, he was waiting by the door, relief in his eyes when he saw me. "You okay?"

"I will be."

"Did you . . ." He didn't need to finish the question for me to know.

"I didn't break up with him," I said. "I couldn't. But it's going to be okay."

"Emma—"

I squeezed his wrist. "I'm going to take care of it."

By lunch, everything seemed oddly normal. Our only

problem was where we should all meet up for prom pictures a week from Saturday.

I realize Mrs. Hobbs is still waiting for an answer. "He's been acting strangely the past few weeks," I say. "Not like himself at all."

"In what way?" Mrs. Hobbs asks.

"He gets angry. But not . . . normal angry . . . He . . ." She's staring so intently I look down at my feet. At my beige sandals on the beige carpet. "He punched his elbow into his truck. He got into that fight with Jace." I look up at her again. "You were there. You saw."

"It was a game. It was the heat of the moment."

"But it was Jace. His best friend."

"Friends get into scuffles all the time."

"It wasn't a scuffle, Mrs. Hobbs." Tears press behind my eyes. "He didn't hurt himself last night slicing an apple. He did it on purpose. He cut his own hand until I promised not to go to Rome."

"Dear God." The blood rushes from her face. Her hand covers her mouth.

"And it's not the first thing he's done to hurt himself. He spilled wax on his arm." Tears overflow with the relief of saying all of this out loud. I brush them away with my fingers. "He needs help, Mrs. Hobbs. I don't know what to do. I've never seen him like this before, and I was hoping you would know. That maybe he's done something like this before—"

"Hurt himself?" she says, interrupting. "No. Never."

"But he told me that you took him to a therapist."

She looks startled. "It was just an evaluation."

"You must have seen something. I thought maybe—"

"It was precautionary. His father had just died." Her hand flutters in the air and makes me think of a hummingbird, not sure where to land. "He was always sensitive, and to lose a father like that at the age of fifteen . . . of course he went through some . . . struggles . . . but he was fine."

"What does that mean? What kind of struggles?"

"Nightmares. Some outbursts. The psychologist said he needed stability, a sense of safety. And he had that, and he was fine." Her eyes narrow with accusation. "He was fine until you told him about that internship."

"What? No." I fight for breath. I want to stand up and shout at her. I want to tell her she's wrong and it's not my fault. But deep down a part of me wonders, *What if it is?* For almost two years I've lived with the guilt of what happened with my family—what I saw, what I said, started it all. Have I somehow done it again? Would none of this be happening if not for me?

"Dillon needs stability, Emma. He needs love. Understanding." She moves from the chair to sit beside me. There's mascara smeared under her eyes now and I can see all the tiny lines around her mouth. Her lips are trembling and there's so much fear in her gaze I have to look away. Instead of regal Mrs. Hobbs, she's suddenly a too-thin woman who looks dazed. "Do you love him, Emma? You've always said you love him."

"I do."

She reaches for my hand. Her skin is thin and cool—mottled with age spots. The bones pronounced. An old hand. A weak, grasping hand. I shudder and she grips me tighter.

"When you first started dating, I warned him about you. Did he ever tell you? I said to him, 'Be careful. She has no stable home life. She'll break your heart.' And you know what he said?"

I shake my head.

"He said, 'No, Mom. She understands what it means to be left. She would never do that to me. The same way I would never do that to her.'"

I pull my hand free and shift away from her on the couch. "I wasn't trying to leave him. It was only an internship."

"Not for him," she says. "For other boys, yes. Other boys would drive you to the airport and wish you well. But you didn't choose other boys. You chose my son, and Dillon can't survive another goodbye right now."

I nod emphatically. "That's why he needs help."

She slides closer again. "And we'll help him, however we can. But you have to be there for him. Give him time to work through this."

"What if it happens again?" I cry. "What if I can't save him?"

"You can." Her voice is low and intense. "You have to love him that much."

I move to slide away from the pleading in her eyes, but I'm at the end of the couch, pressed against the arm.

"You're not like your mother, are you, Emma? You wouldn't walk out on someone who loves you. Who needs you?"

Her words sting like a slap across my face. How dare she—she doesn't know the first thing about my mother. But she's also chosen the perfect words. Because I'm not like my mother. *I can't be like her—not if I want to live with myself.*

"I'll contact the doctor," she says, and there's new strength in her voice. "I'll talk to him and we'll make a plan. But for now, I need you to do this one thing. Stay. I know it's a big thing. I understand that. But if he can regain his balance, then everything will fall into place. Can you do that, Emma? Can you help me take care of him? Both of us, together?"

Slowly, I nod. *Just this one thing. I can do this one thing for Dillon.*

She reaches forward and pulls me into a hug. I feel us, bone against bone. Two skeletons, brittle and breakable. "We're family now, Emma. More than ever."

Fresh tears well up, hot and full. I don't know if I'm crying for Dillon or for me or for the internship. No, not the internship. One day that will hurt, but right now I can stand to watch it die.

Dreams don't bleed.

33

It's all been arranged. I sent Mrs. Lyght an email last night so she's expecting us before first period this morning. It won't take long and then it'll be over.

"Emma!"

Startled, I turn around and see Jace jogging through the parking lot toward me. I'm standing by the flagpole in front of the school, and it reminds me of the other morning when he was waiting for me. That feels so long ago. His backpack bounces against him loud enough to make a smacking noise, but he doesn't slow down. The sky is gray behind him, the sun blocked by thick clouds. The air has that heavy feeling like a monsoon storm is brewing.

"I've been wanting to tell you. I read your essay about the serpent ring," he says, breathing hard as he reaches me. "It's killer, Em."

It takes me a minute to remember that I wanted a fresh set of eyes to read through my application, so I emailed it all to

Jace on Monday before the baseball game. It's like time split in two from the moment Dillon pulled out that knife two days ago. Everything else is Before. And this is After. Jace, with a purple cheek and a split lip, is After.

"I mean really good," Jace says. "No way you don't get this."

I glance out at the parking lot. Dillon dropped me up front and went to park. He likes the far corner—less chance of door dings. As if Jace knows who I'm looking for, his voice lowers and he says, "It's fine, Em. We talked. We're cool now."

"About the application," I say. "Delete it."

"What do you mean, delete it?"

"I'm not going to apply."

His face pales. "What? Why wouldn't you? Your app is amazing. You have to turn it in."

"I've decided not to."

Above my head the flag is flapping and snapping in a stiff breeze. Jace steps closer, ducking his head so his brown eyes can really look into mine. "Even if you want to defer, you still need to—"

"I'm pulling out," I say sharply. "Dillon and I are going to tell Mrs. Lyght this morning."

His gaze shifts and I know Dillon must be striding toward us. "Is he making you do this?" He lowers his voice. "Emma, don't."

"It's done."

I turn as Dillon walks up and give him a smile. Leaves skitter over the pavement and around our feet. "Hey," Jace says, barely meeting Dillon's eyes. The tension is as heavy as the air, filled with the threat of a different kind of storm.

"Hey," Dillon replies.

"Well." Jace shifts his pack to the other shoulder. "I'll let you guys go," he says, then looks at me pointedly. "Run tomorrow?"

"Emma's driving in early with me," Dillon says. "Friday, too."

I am?

"Saturday?" Jace asks.

I slide a hand around Dillon's waist. "Okay. Sure."

Jace nods, hesitating as if he wants to say something else. But Dillon drapes an arm over my shoulder and tugs me into movement. "Later," he says without turning.

As we walk toward the main doors, I can feel Jace watching us and I wish I could stop and go back. Go back to Before . . . I'm so focused on that thought that at first I don't really hear Dillon. "I don't think that's such a good idea."

"What?" I tense beneath the weight of his arm.

"You guys running together. I don't think that's a good idea."

My mouth drops open but I'm speechless. It feels like the alphabet is floating in front of my eyes and I have to pick my words carefully. "We've been running together for a year."

"But things are different now."

A tiny beat of fear pulses in my throat. "I thought you guys were okay."

"Yeah, we are." He squeezes my shoulder.

"Then—"

"Just for a little while. Okay?" He tilts his head and gives me a little smile. "Will you do this one thing for me?"

One thing. His mother's voice echoes in my head. "I already told him I'd meet him Saturday morning, but that'll be the last time. I'll let him know then."

He drifts a kiss over my temple. "If that's what you want."

A scream works up my throat and I bite it back.

Dillon needs me right now. He needs to feel secure—shouldn't I be able to give him that?

Mrs. Lyght smiles when we walk in, but I see the question in her eyes as she adjusts her glasses. "Good morning," she says.

Dillon looks around. He's never been in here, and it's a pretty cool room. Three walls are decorated with a timeline of the world's history. It starts in the corner by Mrs. Lyght's desk with TIME and EVENT and is rolled out like a long scroll of parchment with dates and places printed in black script. Above and below, she's tacked up pictures of people and events that correspond to the times. My seat is in the front row but at the opposite side of the room, where the timeline ends. I sometimes daydream about what will come next. In a hundred years, what will be on the wall? Who will have been important enough to earn a spot?

"You must be Dillon," Mrs. Lyght says, and the future and the past dissolve into the present.

"Hi," he says.

I've always been so proud to introduce Dillon as my boyfriend. I love the impressed look on people's faces when they know that this smart, athletic guy with the compelling eyes and sexy smile is mine. Now I can barely meet Mrs. Lyght's gaze.

"I came to tell you that I've decided not to apply for the internship," I say. I wince at the sound of her disappointed gasp. "Thank you," I force myself to add. "For thinking of me. It means so much, but . . ."

"But?" she asks.

Dillon squeezes my fingers. "But I've decided to stay here next fall. I've already made so many plans."

"I see," she says evenly. But the pinched look at the corner of her mouth says she doesn't see at all. "Have you spoken to your father about this?"

"Her father wants what Emma wants," Dillon says.

Tension crawls over my skin as they stare at each other.

"Anyway," I say. "Thank you again."

"Of course." Mrs. Lyght nods. "If that's your decision, Emma, I'll respect it. You know the application is not actually due until Monday, so if you change your mind—"

"She won't." Dillon smiles as if he's relaxed, but his fingers are vibrating against mine, pressing in and out like some kind of machine.

The early bell rings, startling all of us. "I better get to my locker," I say. "I'll see you later in class."

Outside the room, Dillon and I both let out a breath. "She's probably calling your father right now," he says.

"It doesn't matter," I say numbly. "It's done."

He pulls me into his arms as the hallway begins to fill. "I need to go," I say.

"I know that was hard for you."

"It's okay." I sound like a kindergarten teacher. "There will be other opportunities."

"I'm going to make it up to you." He lets go and I step

back. "You'll still have history, but I'm going to give you the future, too."

"You don't—"

"Shh," he says, cutting me off. He grins. "That's a great line. Let me walk off to it."

He backs down the hall, his eyelids half closed. My beautiful boyfriend in jeans and a gray V-neck and a suggestive smile. I can hardly stand to look at him.

It's like a dust storm has passed and we've put all the furniture back, swept everything clean. The air is clear. But once you've seen what can happen, do you ever forget?

I think of Mount Vesuvius and how the volcano destroyed entire cities. It wiped out thousands of lives, not once, not twice, but many times. Even today, Vesuvius is active and a million people live in Naples, Italy. Willingly. Knowing what they know. They live in its very shadow.

I once asked Dad how people could do that. He got that dreamy look in his eyes as he said, "Behind every shadow lies the sun."

34

Jace is waiting when I get to the trail Saturday morning. His hair is mashed under a black cap, but I'd recognize his shoes anywhere—they're the neon green ones from the day we all met.

"You okay?" he asks as I jog up.

It's another cloudy day, but the sun is making an effort and hazy light streaks over the hills.

"I've been better." I tighten the rubber band around my ponytail. "I thought I looked like total hell, but that was before I saw you."

"You don't like the color of my bruises?"

The swelling of his lip has gone down but there's a black stripe where it's scabbed over, and the bruise across his cheek is softening from purple to a yellowish green. "Does it hurt?"

"Only when I press on it to see if it still hurts."

I smile and start down the path at a slow jog. Jace slides

in beside me, the smell of his soap so familiar it's like a part of the trail.

"I'm listening," he says. "In case, you know, you want to talk."

"Let's see," I say with fake cheeriness. "Should we talk about my dad, who's been working for two weeks on a memory book for the woman who left him? Should we talk about how I have to deliver the book today and have lunch with my mom and her new family?" I drag in a tight breath. "Should we talk about my sister, who I've been dodging and who thinks it's because of my dad but doesn't know the half of it? Or how about my friend Marissa, who I've let down, again, and Sarah, who thinks I'm a crappy friend and as it turns out is right? Or how about the internship I just passed on? What should we talk about, Jace?" I sound as out of breath as if we're sprinting and not jogging. I also sound bitter and whiny. I'm a little ashamed that I'm taking this out on him. He's been a good friend, and the truth is I don't know what I'd do without him.

"Did I say talk?" Jace deadpans. "Because quiet is good. I like quiet."

I smile and let some of my tension go as my breath settles into an easier rhythm. "I love those shoes," I say.

"Good memories, huh?" I feel the smile in his words.

"The best."

The mourning doves are up ahead again, crying, their brown chests just visible behind the leafy screen of the tree.

"Why do they call them mourning doves?" I ask.

"Probably because they're the most hunted bird in America."

I turn to look at him, surprised. "Are they really? How do you know that?"

"Dillon told me," he says. "His father took him bird hunting a few times."

"Of course," I mutter.

"We have to talk about him, Emma."

"Do we?"

Jace sighs. "He's freezing me out. Pretends like everything is fine, but if I even mention your name, he cuts me off."

I duck to avoid an overhanging branch. "He doesn't want me to run with you anymore."

"What?" He turns sideways to stare at me and then stops altogether. "Emma!"

I stop, too, kicking at the knotted stump of a broken branch before turning to face him. "He cut himself, Jace. On purpose."

His mouth drops open. "What! My God. You're sure?"

"Yeah." The horror is back, just with that one word.

Ahead of us, two older ladies appear, one walking a small black dog with a red polka-dot leash. He curses under his breath and gestures to the trail. We jog again, passing the ladies. When the trail is clear ahead, he says, "You should have told me. We have to do something. We have to tell someone."

"I did. I told his mom."

"And?"

"And it's covered."

"Covered?" He stops again.

Sighing, I slow to a stop and turn. "What?"

"What the hell does that mean, covered?"

"His mom is going to talk to a doctor."

"She's going to talk to someone?" His voice rises. "What if he tries something . . . does something . . . What if—"

"It's okay. He's not going to do anything like that again."

"How can you be sure?"

"Because I gave up the internship."

He plants his hands on his hips and stares at the dirt. "Aw hell, Emma."

I clench my jaw, very close to lashing out again. "A second ago you wanted to get Dillon help. This is what will help." I turn back to the trail and start running.

"Emma, come on!" His voice is frustrated. Does he think he's the only one?

He catches up and reaches for my arm. "There has to be something else we can do."

I stop and shake my arm free. "There isn't."

"So that's it? You're just going to give up everything?"

"I'm not giving up everything. Right now, he needs this. He needs me. You know he hasn't been himself this semester. You said it yourself. But it's not going to go away or work itself out. He needs counseling. Once he's stronger, then I can think about Rome again."

He pulls off his hat and runs a hand through his matted hair. "I can't believe this is happening. This is Dillon we're talking about. Dillon!"

I shrug. I don't know what to say.

"Maybe if I stay. If I take the Bergen Scholarship—"

"Jace—"

"No," he snaps. "You shouldn't have to do this!"

Frustration hums between us and we both turn back to

the trail. This wasn't a good idea—running with Jace. It's only making things harder. The path winds right and circles a giant rock outcropping. I usually love this part of the trail. It's shaded and cool, dipping beneath the branches of three trees that form a canopy. Today it feels more like a tunnel—dark and claustrophobic.

"It's not that big a deal," I say. "Think about all the sacrifices people make for love. How many kids do we know who are choosing universities because of a boyfriend or a girlfriend? They're going to move across the country and rack up huge debt all so they can be near the person they love. Look at everything my dad has been going through, all for the sake of love. Me, I'm sacrificing an *internship* that I probably wasn't going to get anyway."

The trail rises over a muddy patch of rock but jutting from beneath a ragged boulder is a spray of wildflowers. It's beautiful and harsh all at the same time. Like life, I think.

"So," I say, "we'll skip a few runs, wait a week or two, and then I'm sure things will get back to normal."

"Normal, huh?"

"I have to do this, Jace. When you love someone, you have to help them—any way you can."

"Yeah," he says, a funny note in his voice. "I guess you do."

"So we'll just be patient for a little while."

"Emma." He stops so suddenly I don't realize it at first. It's his voice that makes me turn to him. I wait as he walks toward me, his breath coming in short, fast bursts. At first I think he's reacting to what I've said, but then I see that his gaze is lifted to one of the hills that overlooks the trail.

"What?" I say, even as I'm searching to figure out what

has him so stiff. All I see is the rising slope of the peak. Then something flashes in the sun. A pair of sunglasses. There's someone sitting on top of the hill. It's too far away to see clearly, but I know.

The sweat on my skin turns into chills. Dillon is watching.

35

When I get home from my run, Dad is sitting at the kitchen counter sipping a cup of coffee. He's dressed in a deep pink polo I've never seen before and the jeans that Lauren and I tease are his "sexy jeans" because they have embroidered pockets and a fitted cut. His hair is still damp from a shower and carefully brushed forward.

"Dad!" I don't know what to say. I'm not sure why he's up this early or why he's dressed like this or why he seems so bright-eyed. But I feel as fragile as a fossil, and the only thing I'm absolutely sure of is that I'm not going to like it and I can't deal with it right now.

"Did you have a good run?" he asks.

I open the fridge and reach for a cold bottle of water. "Um. Yeah." I unscrew the cap and take a deep drink, feeling the cold work its way to my stomach. I still feel an itch between my shoulder blades as if Dillon is watching me. "I'm going to get in the shower," I say.

"Sounds good." His smile seems a little forced. "Then I'll tell you about the great idea I had last night."

"Dad—"

"I'm going with you today to see Mom. I should be there when she opens her present."

My gaze shifts to the album that is now wrapped in silver paper and tied with every color of ribbon we own. Dad runs a finger over the edge of one ribbon. "You would have laughed if you'd seen me trying to make these curlicues. I couldn't figure how to hold the scissors. So much for my advanced degrees."

I close my eyes against his sweet smile. "We already agreed that I would bring it to her. Remember? Give her some time to look at it without feeling pressured."

"There's no reason for her to feel pressured."

"Look at you," I say. "Is that a new shirt?"

He looks down at himself. "What's wrong with trying to look nice?"

"Because she's going to know that it's all part of a manipulative plan to get her to take you back."

He blinks, startled. "Polo shirts are not manipulative."

I rub the cold bottle over my hot forehead. "Just let me go by myself. Please?"

"We have things we should talk over. Your trip to Rome, for starters. She's hurt, by the way, that you've only texted her the basics."

"Because I knew I'd see her today." I take a deep breath. I half expected Mrs. Lyght to tell Dad my decision, but I'm not going to get off that easily. *Oh, why not just get it over with?* "As it turns out, I'm not going to Rome."

He tilts his head as if he didn't quite hear. But he did.

"I've decided to stay here. I'll go to ASU as planned. You've always said you could get me volunteer work close to home. There's the Land of Enchantment in New Mexico, right?"

He cups his hand around his mug but doesn't drink. "When did you decide all of this?"

"The other day."

"And why? There's a copy of your assignment on the home computer. I've read it, Emma. The work you did is excellent."

"I'm not submitting it."

"Of course you are."

"No, I'm not."

"Emma."

I start to go around him toward the hall but he stands and blocks my way.

"Is this because of Dillon?" His eyebrows dip in disgust. "You're not giving up an opportunity like this for a boy. Please tell me that's not what's happening here."

"I'm eighteen, Dad. I'm old enough to make my own decisions."

"Then act like it."

I shake my head, fighting off anger and exhaustion. "I'm going to take a shower."

"We're not done talking."

I push past him. "I am."

"Then I'll have a talk with Dillon."

I spin back around, my heart racing. "No, Dad!"

"He says he loves you. Well . . . if he does, then he won't allow you to sacrifice this internship."

It's all too much then. The mix of anger and fear boils over and comes spewing out in a cry. "What about the sacrifices I made for you? Do you ever think about that? All the school games I missed, the dances and the parties so I could stay with you over the weekends. So I could put you to bed when you got too drunk to do it yourself. I moved across town to take care of you! I was going to be a senior, Dad. I was going to be . . ." I swallow a sob as all the things I was going to be and do flood through me. "And you let me give it all up. You never even said you were *sorry*."

His mouth drops. "You said you wanted to move, to make a new start."

"But I didn't have to move so far away. I wouldn't have left my friends if I wasn't so worried about you." Tears spill down my cheeks and into my mouth. "You were out of control, following Mom. Showing up outside Henry's house. And look at you in your new shirt—like she still might change her mind."

"We had twenty-five years together!" His voice trembles. "You don't understand what that means." He grips the countertop, squaring his shoulders. "We share things she'll never have with that man. *I* was the one who got her through the winter when her brother died. *I* was the one who held her hand when she gave birth to the two of you. *I* was there when she had a cancer scare and when she sold her first house."

"And I was there when she said she was leaving!"

His head bobbles back as if I've just slapped him, and it feels *good*. "She's not coming back," I say. "She sold the house. It's gone. She's not lonely. She's not rattling around in the past like you are. She's with Henry. With his kids. She's gone, Dad, and she's not coming back."

He staggers back a step, then finds his way into the chair at the counter and sits heavily. "She sold the house? She couldn't have. She loves that house. I would know." His voice grows stronger. "I would know."

I stride across the kitchen to where the phone is sitting in its cradle. I grab it and bring it back to the counter. I drop it on the granite with a clatter. "There. Call Lauren if you don't believe me. She's been after me to tell you for weeks, but I didn't want to hurt you. But you can't go to the house today and you can't bring Mom the book because she's not there."

He grabs for the counter as if he's physically going to teeter over. Disbelief flares in his eyes as the muscles of his face sag. He blinks back at me—an old man. Guilt rises, sudden and fierce. *What did I do?* "Dad?" I say hesitantly.

"When did this happen?"

"We packed up the house over spring break."

"And she's been living with him?"

I swallow. "Yeah."

"The house is gone," he says carefully, as if he's testing the words.

"Yeah."

He's quiet for a long minute. "I've seen his boys, you know." Dad shakes his head. "A ten-year-old and a twelve-year-old. Out of control, both of them." He looks at me, his face pinched in disbelief. "I wonder how that's going to work."

I wipe at the wetness under my nose and eyes. "I'll bring her the album, Dad. I know she'll appreciate having it."

"Sure." But I can tell he's not really listening to me. He shakes his head again, lost in his own thoughts. "Day in, day out. She's going to be miserable, and sooner rather than later."

"Dad?"

"I guess we'll see." He straightens and stands. The lost look is gone. There's the hint of a smile on his lips and I can see hope flare as if he's just struck a match to a wick that had burned out. "We'll see."

36

"Grinding has been outlawed." Hannah announces the news as she sits with her tray of pizza and—of course—pork rinds.

"I didn't know you could outlaw a verb," Jace says.

Spence shrugs. "We already have so many of them."

"The dancing kind," Hannah retorts. "In preparation for a prom with no sexual intent or content."

We're sitting at our usual picnic table, though I think this will be our last Friday for that. We're in the second week of April now and even sitting in the shade it's starting to feel a little sticky out here.

"I overheard Mrs. Bishop in the office," Hannah continues as she opens a can of orange soda. "They're going to make the announcement later today."

I smile because that seems like the right thing to do and I've been careful all week to do the right thing. Dillon rubs a hand over my back and I'm careful not to stiffen.

"But that's my best move," Spence complains. "I'm a world-class grinder."

"I thought that was an Italian sub?" Jace quips.

"Idiots," Hannah pronounces cheerfully. "We're meeting at six for pictures, right?"

I nod, looking to Dillon for confirmation. In the end, we decided to all meet for pictures by a man-made lake in Hannah's neighborhood. Then Dillon and I are having a romantic dinner in the guesthouse before the dance—Mrs. Hobbs has it all arranged. It's the first time we'll be alone since the night he cut his hand. His touch feels connected to that night now—to all the blood, to all the fear. *Let's wait for prom,* I said. *To make it more special.* I keep thinking that normal is one more night's sleep away, but it's Friday now and I'm still on edge. I'm careful not to let that show, either.

"I don't want anyone to comment on my dress," Hannah says. "It's Spencer's fault that I'm going to look like a frightened peacock."

"I said I'm going vintage blue. You didn't have to match."

"Of course I have to match. That's one of the key components of prom torture." She looks at Jace. "Is Mel matching?"

Jace is taking Melodie Chung. It all happened last-minute, but Hannah thinks it's romantic. Mel is the student trainer for the baseball team, and apparently she was the first to apply ice to Jace's face. According to Hannah, love is the silver lining to Jace's faded bruise. I'm just happy he has a date, because it might relax Dillon. All I can think about anymore is if Dillon is calm. If Dillon is happy. I've become a human tuning fork. I seem to exist only to pick up on Dillon's moods.

234

It is getting better.

I tell myself this every day.

I love Dillon; he's more important than Rome could ever be.
He saved me and now I can save him.

I tell myself this every day, too.

Just because I gave up this opportunity doesn't mean there won't be others. In fact, I've been thinking I'll talk with Mrs. Lyght again. Tell her to keep me in mind for something next summer.

"Emma!"

I hear my name and look toward the doors to the cafeteria. It's almost as if I've conjured Mrs. Lyght from my thoughts. She smiles and heads toward the table, her slacks flapping she's moving so quickly.

"Do you have a minute?" she asks.

I look down at my half-eaten turkey sandwich. I don't remember tasting the part I did eat. "Sure."

"Looks like some good news," Dillon says.

"As a matter of fact, it is." Mrs. Lyght beams. She slides onto the edge of the bench next to Jace. "I just heard from Dr. Abella in Rome. You've got it, Emma. The internship is yours!"

I hear the words but I can't make sense of them. I feel like a fish with my mouth open, drowning on nothing but air. "What?" I finally say.

"It's yours."

Gazes shift to me and I shake my head. "It can't be," I say. I look at Dillon. His jaw is tight, a muscle twitching in his cheek.

"You applied?" he asks.

"No!" I look at Mrs. Lyght. "It's not possible. I never sent you my application."

"Yes, but . . ." She looks as if she's suddenly feeling my panic.

And then I know exactly what happened. "It was my dad, wasn't it?" I snap. "The application was on his computer. Of course it was him. He has your email—what could have been easier?"

Even behind her glasses, Mrs. Lyght's eyes are wide with denial. "It wasn't your father. It . . ."

Her gaze shifts to Jace. It's not a random look. I stare, slowly processing the pleading in his brown eyes. But I don't want to believe it. I don't want it to be true because then I have to hate the one person I've been depending on.

"I thought you could see how you compared," he says. "Just to know how good you really are."

I can't look at him. I can't listen. "You let him submit it for me?" I say to Mrs. Lyght.

"I'm so sorry, Emma." She presses her hand over her heart. "He said you had a virus on your home computer. And the attachment had your complete application, including the essay. I thought you must have changed your mind, but I never should have—" She swallows the rest of her words as her gaze shifts to Dillon and back to me. "I'm very sorry. Of course I'll inform Dr. Abella of the error."

I'm suddenly aware of Dillon's tension beside me. Is there threat in the way he's holding himself? Is he a fuse that's just been lit or am I imagining it? Does it matter if I am or not? How do I take that risk? "You do that."

She stands. "You should still feel very proud of what you

accomplished. Emma, he said you were the only candidate still in high school and the only one who seemed to grasp what the museum is trying to achieve." She shrugs almost helplessly. "I'm so sorry."

Why is she telling me this? I don't want to hear this! My breath feels as thin as thread. "Thank you."

As soon as Mrs. Lyght is gone, Hannah snaps at Jace. "How could you do that?"

"Seriously, man," Spence adds. "That's effed up."

"Her application was really great. I wanted them to know it." He looks at Dillon and then me. "I wasn't trying to mess things up for either of you."

"But you did," Hannah snaps.

His gaze never leaves Dillon. "She deserves this, Dillon. You know she does."

"It's none of your business," Hannah answers.

He faces her, his face red, and he leans forward. "I'm the one who turned down the internship in the first place because I wanted Emma to have it. It's perfect for her, and everyone should see that!"

"You . . . what?" I hear my own voice as if it's coming from a distance.

Jace's eyes flare with a sudden dawning horror and then his shoulders sag on an exhale. "Shit."

The blood is roaring through my ears. "You what?" I cry.

"Emma, let me explain—"

"It's okay," Dillon says in a low but commanding voice that silences everyone at the table. He surprises me by putting an arm over my shoulder and gently squeezing. I'm shaking and he's strangely calm. "I'm sure Jace meant well."

Warily, I search his eyes for a sign of anger. Instead, he seems almost happy. "I had no idea," I say.

"I know. It doesn't matter."

For some reason, I brace myself. His smile frightens me more than his tension. "You mean that?" I whisper.

"I'm going to make this all okay." His eyes glimmer like tiny blue flames. "You'll see why tomorrow."

Dread sends shivers through me.

"You cold?" he asks. He pulls me closer. "Come here, baby."

Don't call me that! I want to scream.

But I'm careful not to say a word.

37

I study myself in the bathroom mirror and Cinderella stares back. I've turned myself into a fairy princess—at least from the outside. All that's missing is the smile. I've been even more afraid since Mrs. Lyght dropped her little bomb at lunch yesterday. That's how screwed up my world has become. This is the best news I've ever gotten and all I can think about is whether my boyfriend will poke more holes in himself because of it. Is that the wonderful surprise he's got planned for me?

Roses arrived earlier today.

Get ready for a special night.

All along I've been thinking that everything will be okay by prom. But Dillon picks me up in an hour, and my stomach is so twisted I haven't been able to eat since lunch yesterday. I called Mrs. Hobbs. She said Dillon was fine—that he'd been busy on his computer and on the phone making some sort of plans. She told me she'd spoken to the doctor. There was a scheduling snafu but she had a consultation scheduled for next week. She was going to wait and tell him about it after prom. *Everything is all right.*

Still, I lay awake last night, every creak of the house, every hoot of an owl making me jump. My eyes flickered to the window so often I finally turned on the bedside lamp.

I have to get ahold of myself. If Dillon is slipping out of control, he wouldn't be making all these plans, would he? The thought calms me a little—enough to appreciate my reflection. Thank God for salons. Hannah and I met at the neighborhood spa this morning and treated ourselves to manis and pedis, worrying over which shade of polish to choose as if it were the biggest decision in the world. She was sweet with me, almost protective. I'm doing the right thing for Dillon, and she wants me to know it.

From there, we moved to the salon. Sandra, the stylist, grinned when she felt the thickness of my hair and said, "This is going to be fun." Fun turned out to be curling my hair and gathering it in back in a jeweled clip, leaving soft waves to drape over my shoulders and back. I've had my hair in a ponytail so often I hadn't realized how long it's grown. Sandra curled tendrils at my ears and fluffed up my bangs and then she did my makeup.

Even now, with the apricot dress soft against my skin and my hair and makeup done, it's hard to believe this is actually prom. I've imagined this night ever since my freshman year. Marissa and I used to thumb through racks of prom dresses, picking the ones we'd wear while my mom would patiently wait and nod over every frilly gown.

Tears prick my eyes at the memory. Marissa should have been with me today—I should have been with her. Their prom isn't for another week, but I don't even know if they're all going as a group or if she's found a date. I've messed up—so many things I've messed up. I reach for my phone, suddenly knowing that I need to talk to her. I open contacts and hit her name, waiting as the phone dials, nearly breathless to hear her voice.

The call connects. "Hey, Emma."

Not Marissa's voice.

"Hi, Sarah." My eyes close and my head dips. "Where's Marissa?"

"Kitchen. She went to get us sodas."

"Then I'll wait."

"It's not a good time."

"Sarah—"

"It was a good time last week or the week before or the week before or the week—"

I cut her off with a sharp, "I get it, all right? But I need to talk to her now."

There's a frustrated huff of air on the line. "Did it ever occur to you that she might have needed to talk to you over the past *year* when you've been too busy with your boyfriend to make time for her?"

"Sarah."

"I'll tell her you called."

"Sarah—"

The screen flashes. Call ended.

I stare at the phone. I don't know what to do. Should I call back? Should I call Marissa's house phone? I'm like a kid at a birthday party blindfolded and turned around so many times I don't know where to turn. I'm reaching out and grasping nothing but air.

I'm still staring at the phone when it beeps again. I startle, but it's not Marissa. It's a text from Mom.

Can we Skype? I'd love to see your dress—just for a few minutes.

And I type YES because I can't stand feeling this alone. Because after everything, I still want my mom.

When her call rings in on my computer, I hit the video button. My face flashes on-screen and there's an instant when Mom's brows draw in and her smile falters. I can see the question on her face. *Are you okay?* Because even with cover-up and two kinds of de-puffing eye cream, I still look like Tired, Stressed-Out Cinderella. The fact that she sees it— that she knows me that well—brings a lump of regret to my throat. Maybe we'll get back to the point where she can say, "Honey, you look like shit." But right now, she can't. And the expression on her face says she knows it, too.

"Let me see your dress," she asks.

And I move the laptop so she can see the satin bodice and the line of fabric hugging my middle and hips. It was tighter two weeks ago, which makes me realize that I've lost weight.

"What shoes are you wearing?"

"Four-inch heels that you'd hate."

"Ouch," she says, but she smiles. "You'll be as tall as Dillon. Have you talked to Lauren?"

"Not since your birthday. We haven't been able to connect." Truth is, I've been avoiding her calls. She's the one person I can't lie to, and I'm too embarrassed to admit what's happening. Even this past Saturday at Mom's birthday lunch she could tell something was wrong, but I blamed it on the fight with Dad. She was so relieved I'd finally told him that she didn't even ask about Dillon. The subject of Rome turned out to be easy, too. I dodged the whole discussion by saying the application was finished and I didn't want to talk about it. Everyone assumed I was nervous about jinxing my opportunity. Another thing I'll have to explain, but not yet. Not until Dillon has seen someone and I can finish the story with a happy ending.

The silence stretches out and I almost feel sorry for Mom. For a long time, I've wanted her to suffer the way we have, but I'm starting to see that she has. She cried when I brought her the memory book and told her Dad was still holding out hope. I wanted to forgive her then. I almost did and maybe I would have if I hadn't just made a different choice. She should have been strong enough to make the choice I did. To stay.

"Well, I won't keep you," she says. "You look beautiful, honey. Tell Dillon to take care of you tonight and drive safe."

"I will."

"I love you, Emma."

I flush and look down. "I'll send you pictures tomorrow."

When I hear the doorbell a little later, I walk out of my room to find Dad standing in the entryway, holding the door for Dillon. He looks like every girl's prince with his hair gleaming as black as the tux that's fitted over his wide shoulders. His shirt is white with pleats down his flat midriff, and his vest is a glossy charcoal gray. He's holding a wrist corsage of white and peach roses.

"Oh," I say stupidly. "I forgot to get you a boutonniere."

He smiles. His cheekbones are sharper and I know he's lost weight, too. "I don't care about that, Em. It's enough to see you like this. You're beautiful."

"Thank you." His voice is reverent, full of love. This is a night I've dreamed of, and with him standing here like this, I can almost forget about all the other stuff. The blister on his wrist is healed so that it barely shows. Even the bandage is gone from the back of his hand, replaced with a smaller pad over his palm. I remember now that he got his stitches out today.

"You both look wonderful," Dad says. He's beaming at me, and it's as if we've fallen right back into the roles of doting dad and little girl. As if everything is right with the world. For one night I want it to be. I want to ride off in an orange pumpkin and have my magical evening. I want to try to believe in fairy tales again. I lean up and kiss Dad's cheek.

"I'll see you at the lake for pictures," he says.

When Dillon swings open the door of the truck, it smells like vanilla and leather polish, and every surface is shining. "My lady," he says. He sees me struggling with my purse and my skirt and reaches out a hand. "Here, let me take that." He tucks my purse under his arm and takes my hand in his and helps me up, then carefully arranges my skirt around my feet before closing the door.

He's smiling when he climbs in beside me. "Are you good? You comfortable?"

"I'm fine," I say. "The truck looks amazing."

"I want everything to be perfect for you." His eyes lock onto mine. "Tonight is just the beginning."

He shifts the truck into drive, and I spend a minute trying to pull on my seat belt and arrange it so it won't crease my dress. He turns left out of my street and I straighten the wrist corsage, smelling the sweetness of the roses. I'm a little light-headed and realize now I should have had something to eat or drink. When he makes another left, I sit up straighter. "The lake is back that way."

He turns to give me a quick smile. "We're not going to the lake."

My heart revs with the sound of the engine. "Did the plans change? I need to call my dad. He's meeting us over there."

He turns out of the neighborhood and signals for the freeway entrance.

"Dillon?"

"Remember I said I had a surprise? This is it."

He turns onto the freeway. Dread spirals up my spine, tightening every nerve ending. "You said you were all right. You said everything was all right."

"Everything is better than all right," he says. He's thrumming with some kind of manic energy. I look around and spot a small black suitcase on the floor of the backseat. My throat goes dry. "Why is there a suitcase back there?"

"It's part of the surprise."

Panic beats in the pulse of my neck. "Dillon, what's going on?"

"I'm going to make sure no one can ever separate us again."

Sweat dampens my palms as I look at the open highway ahead of us. I lean down for my purse and my cell phone. I brush away my skirts, then turn to face Dillon. "Where's my purse? I need to call my dad."

"I've got it over here." He pats the compartment on his door.

I work to breathe, to keep my voice low and controlled as the miles stretch out behind us. "Where are we going, Dillon? Tell me now. I mean it."

"I'm taking you to Vegas," Dillon says. He glances at me, his eyes shining. "That's the surprise. We're getting married tonight."

The words sink in along with the complete certainty in his gaze. My chest convulses and an unhinged sort of laugh bubbles up my throat. He doesn't seem to notice. He laughs, too. I cover my mouth with my hands because I'm going to lose it completely and I can't do that. I'm such an *idiot*. The word rings through my head. I'd nearly convinced myself the surprise would be a sapphire bracelet to match the earrings he'd given me at Christmas.

My heart is beating like a bird in a cage. I work to breathe. *Stay calm. Breathe.* "Dillon, no. This is crazy. We're not getting married. We're going to prom. Tonight is prom."

He shifts to the fast lane. "I told you it would be a special night, didn't I?"

I swallow a choked sob as another mile marker flies by outside my window. "I want to go to prom, Dillon. I've never been, and everyone is waiting for us. We're supposed to be at the lake for pictures."

"It's okay. I told Hannah to let the others know that we wouldn't be there."

I grip the handle of the door as he takes the overpass heading west. "It's sweet. Really sweet. But—"

"This will be our prom story," he says. "One day you'll be telling our kids how Dad whisked you away to get married."

Another awful laugh bubbles up, this one sounding more like a cry. "This isn't the right way. When we get married, it'll be with our families there and our friends."

"Our families and friends," he repeats with an edge to his voice. He lowers the visor—we're heading full west now and the sun is sinking. It'll be dark in another hour, and panic spikes at the thought. "Why should any of them be a part of this? They don't understand. They think you're giving up your future for me. They don't get that we're committing ourselves to a future together."

I shake my head but he doesn't see. "Dillon, we don't need to prove anything to anyone."

"I'm not doing this for them," he says, his look full of surprise. "I'm doing this for you. For us. So we'll never have to worry about being parted again."

A green sign flashes overhead. I scan the upcoming exits, but I'm not familiar with this area. Downtown Phoenix is fading away, and instead of strip centers and red-tiled roofs there's more open desert.

"Dillon, stop," I say. "We can't do this."

"That's what I thought at first, too," he says. "But we're both eighteen and the ceremonies in Vegas are completely legal. We'll need to file the paperwork with the state of Arizona, but there's nothing to stop us." He reaches out and

248

curves a finger around a tendril of hair by my ear. I jerk my head away.

"Don't worry, baby. It's all planned out. I found us a little chapel." His eyes glow as he looks at my hair, my dress. "You're going to be the most beautiful bride."

I press myself into the corner of my seat. "You have to stop the truck. This isn't the way to do things."

For the first time a flash of unease crawls over his face. "Did you want a big wedding? I know we talked about it once before and I told you I'd give you your dream."

"Yes," I cry quickly. "I want a fairy-tale wedding, Dillon. With everyone there."

He nods. "We'll do it again, then. A second wedding, just the way you want." His expression softens, turns dreamy. "My mom will love helping you plan it and we'll have all the time in the world. As soon as we have the license, no one can separate us—not even your dad."

He turns up the radio. Bass drums throb from the speakers, beating through me like bursts of fear. I stare through the windshield. The billboards are a blur, the mountains looming in the distance. *How did I get here? How did this happen?*

I think of Dad; I can hear his voice in my head.

We only see once it's too late.

But I know now that he's wrong. We *do* see. We see every damn sign along the way. We choose not to pay attention.

Oh God. I've been so angry with Mom all this time. I could never get past the question of *How do you leave?* I never for a second wondered if the real question was *How do you stay?*

A rolling ball of brambles skitters across the highway, swept ahead of us in an uncaring breeze. My gaze follows it as it bounces across asphalt and into a field of dirt before we've moved too far past for me to see it anymore. I'm being swept along, every bit as out of control as that tumbleweed.

Except that I'm not some dead thing. I have a choice.

An impossible choice.

I blink away tears and draw in a breath. "Stop the car, Dillon. I'm serious." I hold on to the dash with one hand and the edge of his seat with the other. "I'm not doing this. We're not doing this."

"It's the only way," he says.

"But it's not. There are always other ways." I turn off the radio. "Take the next exit."

He's staring straight ahead.

"I'm not marrying you." I raise my voice over the noise of the engine and the rush of air. "Do you hear me?"

The truck jerks as he speeds up. Another exit flies by. "Stop the truck so we can talk!" Fear throbs through my voice. My gaze darts up and back. Where's a cop? *Please, God, let there be a cop!* He hits a pothole and I scream as the truck jumps, yanking my seat belt tight. "Stop it, Dillon!" I yell. "You'll kill us both!"

His fingers whiten as he grips the steering wheel tighter.

"Dillon, you promised you would never hurt me. You promised!"

It's as if he doesn't hear me. What do I do? *Marry him? Do I marry him?*

Blood beats in my ears. "If I'm dead, I can't love you, Dillon." The words fly from my mouth, desperate and afraid, but I see his face flicker with doubt. I force myself to shift closer to him. I grip the back of his seat with my hand. "If I'm dead, how can I save you?"

He slants a look at me, his eyes staring. Hopeful. *Happy.* His foot lifts off the gas. The truck stops rattling and bouncing, though the desert is still flying by.

I swallow the urge to be sick. "It's okay, Dillon. We save each other, don't we?"

Sweat shines on his face. "You'll save me, won't you, Emma?"

"Always. Don't I always?" I force a smile. "Pull over, Dillon. I need to hold you. Don't you need to hold me?"

There's no exit in sight, but up ahead the shoulder is wide and flat. Dillon eases the truck into the dirt and pulls to a stop. When he shifts into park, I finally let out my breath.

I sag weakly against my seat. To my right is a wide field of desert scrub and low rocky hills. Behind us a car whizzes by, and then it gets still. Quiet.

I unsnap my seat belt and shift my knee to the seat so I can reach closer to him. I have to pull the dress up to free my legs as I wrap my arms around his neck. I press Dillon back and slide far enough over so that I'm straddling his legs.

"You scared me, Dillon." With one hand I draw circles on his neck. With the other, I reach for my purse and clutch it in my fingers.

"I didn't mean to," he says. "I only want us to be together."

I grip him tightly for a second, fighting tears. Then I climb off his lap and take the truck keys in one quick motion.

His eyes flash in surprise.

"I'm going to get you help."

"What? No!" He reaches for me, but his seat belt is still attached and yanks him back.

I shake my head as I reach for the door. "You're not okay, Dillon. You don't see it because you're not thinking straight right now, but I'm going to do everything I can."

The door clicks open and warm desert air rushes in. Desperation flashes in his eyes. "Don't leave me, Emma. You can't leave me." He lifts the console and pulls out his father's knife. *Oh God, I should have looked for the knife!* With a quick motion, the sheath flies onto the dash and the blade gleams.

I hold up my hands. "Dillon, no. Just be calm. I'm going to call for help. Okay?" I let the tears run down my face unchecked as I fumble to open my purse.

"I'll be dead before anyone can get here."

"No. Don't say that. You don't mean that." I struggle to draw breath, panting for air like someone with asthma. My gaze blurs and some part of my brain recognizes that I'm hyperventilating. I feel around my purse until my shaking fingers find my cell phone. "No knife. Please. I can't breathe."

"It's whatever you want, Emma. I'll do whatever you want."

"I want the knife."

"We're connected, you and me. My blood is your blood. Your blood is mine. As long as we go together."

Oh God.

He's smiling. His skin is stretched tight over his cheekbones. His eyes sunken, dark-rimmed, and mad.

I turn away and stumble out, my dress tearing loudly under my heels. "I'm sorry. I'm so sorry," I cry. He's staring at me. A stranger. And the only boy I've ever loved.

As he presses the knife to his forearm, I stagger away and dial 911.

39

Saturday night is still a blur. Flashes of it come to me when I close my eyes, which is probably why I haven't slept much in two nights. The strange thing is what I remember—odd details as if even my unconscious mind is afraid to go back inside the truck.

I remember the first faint glimmer of red and then the growing sound of the siren a heartbeat later. The shock of the wind grabbing hold of my dress as the paramedics raced past. I remember suddenly feeling my feet and the sting of asphalt on my bare soles. Were my shoes still on the side of that highway? What about my hair clip? Did I lose it then—or sometime later?

I don't remember passing out. I woke in a police car and I remember seeing the wrist corsage and not knowing what it was for one blissful second. I remember Mom and Dad at the hospital and Robin, our police liaison.

The doctor wanted to give me an IV. I was dehydrated,

which was why I'd fainted. I wanted to go home, and Mom said I could. I'd forgotten that the home inside my head wasn't mine anymore.

I remember Mrs. Hobbs rushing in, crying for her son, and I will never forget the hatred in her eyes when she spotted me in a corner of the reception area. I've never felt that cold before. I wonder if that's when my heart froze. Or maybe it turned to ice when I climbed out of Dillon's truck and left him.

"This is not your fault," Mom said. "This is not your responsibility. You did the only thing you could."

So many words. All of them meaningless while we waited for the ones that would matter. The ones about Dillon. I thought the hardest part was not knowing, until I finally learned the truth. That was almost worse.

Dillon was going to pull through. He was going to be okay. He should have died—he would have. But before he'd cut open his vein, he'd taken the time to unbutton his dress shirt and roll up his sleeve. He'd taken the time to carve the name EMMA on his arm.

I'm floating on a pink raft. The sun is bright overhead and the waves ripple beneath me. Dillon is beside me, floating on a white raft. His face peaceful, his hand relaxed as it trails through the pool and droplets of water trickle off his fingers with a soft *drip, drip, drip.*

Not water.

Blood.

Ruby red in sapphire blue. Blue like his eyes. Open eyes that are staring but not seeing.

I jerk myself awake from the nightmare. It's the same one I have every time I drift into sleep now.

Lauren stirs beside me on my bed. "It's okay, Em. You're okay." I hear rustling and she hovers above me with a glass of water. "A sip? Or can I get you to eat some soup?"

I shake my head. I'm still not hungry, but I've given up fighting over liquids. Lauren's been pressing me to drink every half hour for two days and won't budge until I do. She drove up from Tucson yesterday and slept with me last night like when we were little kids.

I take a mouthful of water and hand her back the glass. I don't know what she sees in my eyes because she quickly says, "You're okay. Dillon is okay."

I picture his arm marked forever with my name.

"You want to talk about it?" she asks for the hundredth time. "It's not good—keeping it all inside."

My mind keeps tripping up on the words. What exactly am I keeping inside? Disgust? Horror? Guilt? I don't feel any of it, though I know it must be there, caught beneath the cold numbness.

It's Monday afternoon and we've moved from the bed to the couch and back to the bed. The blinds are closed, so my room is dim. I want to escape into sleep, but I'll only dream again. I sigh. Maybe Lauren is right. She usually is.

"You know how I got him to stop the truck?" I say. "By telling him I'd take care of him. I promised to save him and then I saved myself."

"You didn't do this to him, Em. You're not the bad guy."

"Neither is he," I cry. "He didn't mean to hurt me—that's not what he wanted."

"But he did."

I shake my head.

"He did, Emma."

Her voice is so low it slides in under my guard. With it comes images. I squeeze my eyes shut but I can't stop them: The wax. The blood on my legs. The truck bumping wildly over the highway. The knife pressed against his skin. My breath trembles; my body begins to shake. *How could he do those things?*

"Emma?" Lauren asks. The bed creaks and shifts and then she's up on her knees, wrapping her arms around my shoulders. "I'm here."

"It wasn't fair to make me be the one." I shudder. "To expect me to save him. To force me . . . to force me . . ." I think of that night in the back of his truck and I hate him. I hate that he put me in that position, that I had to give him that, accept that.

And then the sobs begin, because I hate myself, too. I hate myself for going along with it, for letting him do what he did. For not saying no.

I never said no.

Lauren's arms tighten around me, a heavy weight as she rocks with me, holding me together, her words sure and steady. "It's not your fault. It's not your fault."

But how much happened because I let it happen?

What could I have stopped by saying *stop*?

"I thought it was love," I say through my tears. "I thought, how could it be bad—it's love and love is good. Love is supposed to be good, isn't it?"

"That wasn't love," she says.

She hands me a tissue and then another and I press them to my eyes to make the tears stop. "Love screws everything up. It makes us idiots—you've said that before."

"You can't go by anything I say." She holds out the tissue box again and I shake my head. "I watch *Divorce Court* for fun." She sets down the box and adjusts the pillow behind me as I lean back. "I want you to listen to me, Em. Are you listening?"

She waits until I nod. "You can't give up on love. What happened with Dillon wasn't love. That wasn't even Dillon. He's sick right now—suffering from depression or some kind of mental illness. I'm no expert, but what he did—the way he hurt himself—it's not the way a healthy person acts." She presses the heel of her hand over her temple. "I've read so much in the past couple days. There are mood disorders and thought disorders and reactive disorders. I don't know what Dillon has, but the thing is, a lot of it can be treated, you know? He can come out of this and be okay. But he needs professional help. It's not something you could have fixed."

"But he'll always be scarred."

"And so will you," she says bluntly. "But you have to remember that you tried, and because of you he has a chance to be okay. Both of you do." Her voice rises, every word full of fire. "What you did in that truck *was* an act of love—for yourself. You're allowed to love yourself."

"Then why does it feel like it's all my fault?"

"Because you've watched too many bullshit movies that romanticize sacrifice. You were turning yourself into a stump."

"A what?" I shift, sitting up higher.

"You remember that book we read when we were kids? The tree that loved the boy so much that it gave him food and shelter and when the boy needed wood for a house, it gave its limbs and on and on. Until finally the boy had everything and the tree was just a stump."

"Is that the message you took from that book?"

"Yes," she snaps. "It's a classic dysfunctional relationship.

The boy takes and takes and never even thanks the tree until the tree is a dried-up stump, too stupid to realize that it just sacrificed its life for an ingrate. I tell you what, if that tree were a human, it would have been a woman."

I laugh. I can't help it. "It is a woman in the book."

"See!" she cries. "I'm right again." Her voice softens. "You are not a stump, Emma. You are a smart, caring, beautiful, generous human being and, yes, you have a lot to give, but don't sacrifice who you are. Not for anyone or anything. Not even for love."

I can't say anything or I'll cry, but I think of the *Twilight* poster on her old ceiling and that makes me smile. "It was much simpler when love meant a werewolf with nice abs."

She twists so she's facing me, her legs crossed under her. "I think you should talk to someone."

"I'm talking to you."

"A therapist, I mean. Someone objective who can help you through this. Mom agrees. She's going to arrange it."

"You talked about it with Mom?"

"And Dad. All at the same time and in the same room. So see, just talking about therapy has already resulted in a breakthrough."

I smile even as I'm shaking my head.

"I'm being trained to argue for a living," she says. "You won't win." Then she reaches over and squeezes my hand in hers. "Please?"

I worry my teeth over my bottom lip. "Once," I say.

"Once," she agrees. Then she smiles. "To start." She squeezes my hand again and I squeeze back.

"And one other thing." Her chin tilts with determination.

"I want you to come and live with me. You only have another month of high school to finish up, and then you can move to Tucson for the summer and go to U of A in the fall. I can help you get registered and choose classes—whatever you need. It'll be good for you to get away. Think about it," she adds.

I let my eyes drift shut. "I will."

The appointment is Wednesday morning with a therapist named Barbara Caye. I don't want to go. I don't want to relive all of it again, and especially not with a stranger. But I go because Lauren wants me to and because I want someone to tell me what to do—how to live with what's happened.

An hour later, I feel like all I got was some really bad green tea.

Barbara says she's there to listen, as if that isn't the least she can do but the most. And she does listen, gathering up my words as they spill out, defusing them with her nods and knowing eyes.

But she can't give me answers. Not even at the end when I stand up and ask her to please tell me where I go from here. What do I do now? I think maybe that's the moment. She goes to her desk and writes something out on a pad and hands me the slip of paper.

Four words.

WHAT DO YOU WANT?

A question, not even an answer. And not exactly earth-shaking. It's not the kind of thing you expect from someone with umpteen years of education and experience. But I smile and thank her and then I throw the note in the trash outside her office building. I mean, it's the kind of question they ask you in the drive-thru of the taco shop.

But as I drive home, the words keep circling around my mind.

What do I want?

When I get home, Dad is waiting. Sun streams through the kitchen window, painting a long stripe of bright light across the oval table and onto the floor. In another month we'll have to close the curtains during the heat of the day or the kitchen will feel like an oven. Another month. I can't imagine another month anymore. I can't imagine it without Dillon.

Dad has taken the day off and his face is rough with gray stubble, but he's tapping his fingers on the counter and I can tell he has some news.

"How was it?" he asks as I set down my purse.

"It was good."

"Good?" He looks anxious, so I add, "I'm okay, Dad."

Lauren went back to Tucson yesterday morning, so it's just the two of us. As if he can make up for lost time, he's gone into Super-Dad mode, stocking the house with my favorite food and going out to buy a VHS player last night so we could watch the collection of old movies I loved when I was little.

"October Sky," Dad said last night, pulling out a title from the stack.

"We can watch it online," I said, but he wouldn't hear of it and we had a daddy-daughter movie night with popcorn made on the cooktop and the whir of the VHS tape and a grainy picture.

"Buried treasure," he said as we sat on the couch, the same quilt pulled over our legs. It was pretty much perfect.

But it's Wednesday now and I should be back at school. I would have gone back today, but the appointment with Barbara seemed like a good reason to put it off. I don't want to face school. I don't want to face everyone there or feel the absence of the one person who won't be.

"Is everything okay?" I ask Dad now. "You're tapping the counter like you're ready to explode."

He smiles. "I have something to tell you. Come sit?"

I settle myself on a barstool and he sits on the one beside me.

"I checked in with Mrs. Lyght," he begins. "I thought that maybe . . ." He pauses. "The internship is no longer available. Dr. Abella awarded it to another applicant just as soon as Mrs. Lyght gave him your answer last Friday. But," he adds, "I've spoken to a colleague who's leading an excavation project at the Land of Enchantment this summer. He has a spot for you, beginning at the end of May. You'll be close enough to home that you can come back whenever you want and Mom and I can come up for visits. I've even looked into apartments."

"Dad—"

"Please," he says. "Let me do this much. I want to."

I smile, not sure what to say.

What do I want?

The question is still echoing in my head when I head out for an afternoon run. Usually I run to escape my thoughts, but today I need to face them.

I check my watch as I turn onto the trail. It's 2:30 and school will be out soon. Right now I would be packing up in chemistry so I'd be ready when the bell rang. So I could be the first one out of class and hurrying toward the gym to meet Dillon for a quick kiss before baseball practice. I'd see Spence and Jace. They'd all joke about something while Dillon laced his fingers in mine and sighed as if it had been too long since we'd last touched, as if he'd missed me in the two hours since lunch. "Later," Dillon would say, and I'd nod because there was always a later with us.

Always.

What do I want?

I'm beginning to think Barbara Caye is smarter than I suspected.

I jog past the trees and listen for the mourning doves, but even they're silent, probably hiding from the heat. Only the lizards are out, quick slashes of tails like blips in my peripheral vision. I feel tired and slow, but it's still good to be out here. I don't think I've taken a full breath since prom . . . since before that. Since the night he dripped hot wax on his skin. I tense at the thought, waiting for the sickening rush of memory . . . but when it comes it's more like a soft wave, rolling over me and then receding.

I was worried that retelling it all this morning would only make it fresher in my mind. But I suddenly think of Dad and a lecture I once heard him give. He told a hall full of students that the archaeologist bears witness to history. The archaeologist records it and validates it so that the world may move forward. I wonder if that's what Barbara did for me today. If she bore witness to my history.

Will I be able to move forward now?

What do I want?

Barbara's words repeat with every thump of my shoe on the trail. Jace would say it's like a Jedi mind trick.

But I don't want to think about Jace.

I speed up, wanting to leave him behind, but he's already everywhere on this trail, his footsteps an echo in my memory, his laugh, his solidness. He and I talked about this on the hill that day. About what we wanted—for ourselves. He understood me.

He lied to me.

I'm such a mess—torn and bleeding from a million places, and Jace is a wound that's untended . . . festering . . . but I can't face it, or him. Not yet.

267

Not yet.

Do I want Tucson?

New Mexico?

Mom?

She's been calling every day, and yesterday she asked me to consider moving in with her and Henry for the summer. "A change of scenery," she said. "I know you miss Marissa." That much is tempting. I can be the friend I should have been . . . see if that's even possible. "Think about it," Mom said.

So many different ways to go and while it's my choice, are any of them what I would choose?

No.

The answer comes that quickly, that simply. *No.*

What would I choose?

That's ridiculously easy, too.

My breath shudders in and out with the first tentative flutter of possibility. And fear. Because if it's my decision, if I choose . . .

Suddenly, the ground slips away. My shoe skids off a jutting rock and I lurch forward. My arms fly out for balance and my feet skip unevenly until the tread of my shoe catches solid ground. My arms prickle with adrenaline, my heart surging in reaction. But I'm fine—I caught myself.

I slow to a walk. As the fear recedes, a grin builds and widens until my cheeks ache with it. *I caught myself.*

Resting my hands on my hips, I wait for my breath to slow and instead feel my heart quicken, impatient. I stretch my arms like wings and circle the trail like an airplane making a U-turn. I know exactly where I'm headed.

It happens quickly after that. It only takes one email to Mrs. Lyght, and by Wednesday evening I have two letters of recommendation. One from her and the other from Dr. Abella. Both recommending that the American University of Rome accept my late registration. I'd already submitted the initial application along with my transcripts and SAT scores. My essays have been ready since spring break. There's no internship, but there's also no reason why I can't attend a year abroad. Mrs. Lyght offers to help in any way she possibly can. She's sorry, she writes. She shouldn't have sent in the application. She blames herself.

I don't know what to tell her. I don't know how to answer the texts from Hannah and Spence. From Jace. Or from Marissa, who heard what happened from my mom, who told her mom. I don't know what I'll say at school tomorrow. I suppose I'll tell everyone it's okay. And then hope that it will be.

Somehow, I get through my first day back at school on Thursday. I can't spend time with Hannah and Spence. They seem to understand. Maybe it's easier for them that way—their loyalties still lie with Dillon.

I don't know what to say to Jace. Or even how to be around him. He must sense that because he keeps his distance. But I'm aware of him, always. Fluttering just out of sight like a mourning dove.

On Friday, I meet with Mr. Diaz, Dillon's coach and guidance counselor, who is so nice I almost cry in his office, and would have, but he makes such a production out of fake coughing that I end up smiling instead. He tells me that Dillon is getting treatment and will finish school off campus. I don't know how Mrs. Hobbs is handling things. I haven't heard from her, and I doubt that I will. The baseball play-offs will start soon but I won't be there to watch. I don't really care one way or the other, and it seems so strange. I think about the girl who jumped up and down on the bleachers less than two months ago. She seems like someone else.

On Saturday morning, I'm sitting at the kitchen counter in my sleep shirt and shorts, eating a waffle, when the doorbell rings. Dad gives me a wink and goes to open the door.

Mom is standing there in a T-shirt, jeans, and her sturdy Velcro sandals, which means she's ready for a day on her feet. "Surprise," she says. "We're going shopping."

Dad invites her in and he's not crumbling into a pile of need. The lines around his mouth are a little white, as if the smile is strained, but he seems okay. They've spent time together the past few days and it's been good for them. For Dad. And also, I think, for me.

"We're shopping for suitcases," Mom tells me.

I set down my fork, my cheeks flushing. "I just found out yesterday. We have until August to buy suitcases."

The email came late yesterday. I've been accepted to the American University of Rome in the fall. There are more forms to fill out and money to pay, but the admissions office welcomes me. *Accoglienza.*

Dad and I celebrated last night with burgers, cupcakes from a mix, and *Searching for Bobby Fischer* on VHS. Lauren is driving up this afternoon and we'll all go out somewhere nice tonight. My choice, Dad said, so of course I picked Italian.

But shopping?

Mom waves off whatever hesitation she sees on my face. "There's a great sale at the mall today. And it'll be fun."

I'm not so dumb that I don't realize why she's really here. It's exactly one week since prom, and it's going to be a hard day after a bunch of hard days. She's giving me something to do—something else to think about.

She's being my mom.

"I'll get dressed," I say, heading toward my room before tears can come.

The mall smells like pretzels—and we start with one, cinnamon and sugar that we rip off in strips and eat on our way to Dillard's. It's strange, sliding back into mom-and-daughter mode after all this time. The past is still the past, but I've changed. I understand things in a way I couldn't before Dillon.

The luggage department is a zoo. There is a big sale, and I'm swept up in talk of spinners versus rollers and what sizes I'll need and should I get a backpack with wheels for weekends trekking through the Italian countryside. I'm telling Mom about the walled cities of Tuscany when I turn and see a whole display of suitcases in a beautiful shade of deep blue. And I start crying.

Even as I shake her off—tell her I'm fine—she leads me away from the crowds to the back corner of the luggage department. She sits me down in the middle of a display of American Tourister cases. It smells funny—musty and plastic—but it's quieter, and the suitcases are like a wall keeping everything else out.

She pulls a suitcase down and sits beside me on the platform. "I wish you could have told me," she says. "I wish I'd been there for you."

She hands me a tissue and I press it to my eyes.

"I never should have left," she adds, "but I was so unhappy. As much as I wanted to, I couldn't fix it." She grips my hand between her own. "But I wasn't choosing Henry over you," she says. "I need you to know that. I need you to understand."

"I do," I say, wiping my cheeks dry. That's what I finally figured out in Dillon's truck. It wasn't that Henry and his kids mattered more.

It was that she mattered, too.

"I'm not okay with what happened," I say haltingly, searching for the right words. "I don't know if I can ever be. But I understand now about choices. Impossible choices."

"I'm so sorry for that." She pulls me into a hug and I hug her back. "I love you," she says.

Before I can reply, there's a shriek. I look up to see a grayhaired man clutching at his heart. "What are you people doing?" he says. "You scared me half to death."

Mom stands and holds out a hand to me. She pulls me up and straightens her purse. To the man she says indignantly, "We're shopping, what else?"

I smile and follow her back to the front. We pick out a set of purple suitcases along with a backpack. When she drops me off at home, I tell her, "Thank you." And I say, "I'll come over next weekend." And I say, "I love you."

A week has gone by, and then another. It's finally May, and if I could make time go by faster, I would.

I sit at the top of the hill on a Sunday, late in the afternoon, and count it all out in my mind. Finals are in two weeks and then graduation. They're like mountains up ahead that I have to climb, but then I'll have nothing but downhill ahead of me.

I'll get through it, day by day, hour by hour. I've got projects to finish up and so much to research about Rome and where I'll be staying. I've already pored over the course catalogs, narrowing down my choices. Everything sounds amazing, even the basic core classes. Lauren is sick of hearing about it and Marissa isn't far behind, though she's too nice to say so. We're talking more often now, and the distance is still there between us but so is our history. I've come to see that friendship is as much a treasure as anything in this world. Ours might be buried under the weight of the past year, but it's not lost. I can still dig it up and piece it together. Will there always be cracks? Probably. But there's no such thing as perfect. I've learned that, too.

When distractions don't work and it all starts to feel like too much, I have my trail runners and the four-mile loop. But I've stopped running in the mornings. I've started running at dusk and I like it better. The paths are mostly empty.

Except for ghosts.

I'm thinking of Jace, or trying not to think of him, when he finds me.

Jace is a slow-moving shadow, climbing the small hill where I'm sitting. It's not the one he and I climbed—that would be too sad. It's already too sad. My breath is short, my muscles tense. When I think of Jace, it's like a knot in my gut, one that I don't want to unravel, afraid of what I'll find.

He hikes up the last few steps, hesitant in his green sneakers. I look away, out to the horizon and a spray of clouds as thin as steam.

"Hey," he says.

"Hi."

His voice is tentative. "How are you doing?"

"Okay." The clouds shift, pulling apart and reconnecting like strands of lace.

"I saw you head up here." I hear his feet shuffle in the dirt. "You don't have to change your schedule, you know. You can run mornings. I've started running streets. I mean, if that's why you're running later." He clears his throat. "Is that why you're running later?"

"Jace—"

"Never mind. Don't answer that." He paces toward the edge of the hill and looks out. In a deep voice, he says, "Space, the final frontier."

I finally look at him. His eyes are puffy and shadowed. He's always been on the thin side, but now his face is sharp angles, his lips pale. Even his hair seems straighter and limp. "My mom keeps telling me to give you 'space,'" he says, using air quotes. "That always makes me think of *Star Trek*, the episodes that start out with William Shatner saying"—he deepens his voice again—"'Space, the final frontier.'" He shakes his head at himself. "So I'm walking around all the time with William Shatner in my head and I can't sleep and I can't eat and I keep thinking, 'Is this what Emma needs? Does she really need *Star Trek*?'"

When his eyes meet mine, a deep well of anger spills open inside of me.

He reads it—he must. He steps back. "Emma, I'm so sorry."

"You lied to me. You went behind my back."

"I know."

"You were my closest friend. You realize that?" My jaw is tight, every word clipped and edged with fury. "The only one I could talk to. I didn't even know how close we were, how much I depended on you until these past weeks. Until I wanted to call you, wanted to run with you, and I couldn't."

"You could. You can."

"No," I say. "I can't. You ruined us, Jace."

He crouches low, his hands in his hair. "Please, Emma. What can I say? Tell me what to say?"

"Nothing. There's nothing you can say." I want to stay mad—the anger makes it easier—but I feel it deserting me, leaving me tired and unbearably sad. "You can't undo what's been done."

"I would, though. It's all I think about." His throat works up and down. "Can I sit? Just for a few minutes?"

I shrug and he sits a few feet away, like I'm a wild animal he doesn't want to frighten.

"Have you talked to Dillon?" I ask.

He shakes his head. "I've talked to his mom. He's in a program, he wants to be, and he's doing okay. Hannah writes him notes, finds him funny cards that she brings to Mrs. Hobbs. Spence writes things, too, but I don't know what to say. Instead, I've been pulling photos out of the old albums. Pictures of him and me at campouts. Playing baseball. Swimming. In zombie Halloween costumes." He gives me a half-smile. "I think I'm trying to remind him that I was a good friend."

"And?"

"I've been too afraid to give them to Hannah yet."

The sun is hovering just above the tree line, as if it's resting there, taking a last look around before giving way to night. He sighs. "I did it for you. You know? Because I wanted you to have the opportunity."

"But that's not the only reason, is it?"

His voice is barely audible. "No." He hugs his hands around his knees. "I did it for myself, too. Because I liked you more than I should have."

"We were friends, Jace. Just friends."

"I know that. I knew you loved Dillon. And Dillon, he's my best friend. I wanted him to be happy. I wasn't trying to screw everything up, but I thought . . ." He takes in a ragged breath. "I thought here's something I can do. Something I can give Emma that Dillon can't."

When he looks up, his eyes are red and wet. "I screwed up. I know that. I encouraged this thing, even though I could see it was tearing Dillon apart. Even though it was tearing you apart."

I squeeze my eyes shut and wipe away tears. When I open them, he's looking into the sky, his face pale and haunted. "The worst part is that I can't seem to stop being in love with you."

I'm breaking apart like the clouds. Adrift. Even my voice sounds faint. "Jace, don't."

"I need to say it. Because I wasn't honest with you and I should have been. I . . . I should have been."

He dips his head, and for a second I see the boy I met last winter running on the trails. I see the messy hair. The warm brown eyes, squinted against the sun. His gangly stride and the way he smiled at me as we met up all those mornings. I see all the things there are to love about Jace.

But I also see the shadow of Dillon.

"I don't want you to love me, Jace," I say. "I don't want anyone to love me or need me like that, not ever again. I don't want to love anyone like that again."

"Emma."

His voice is an ache, and I understand. There's so much pain in loving. Too much. From now on, I'm going to keep my heart safe.

"I should go," I tell him. I stand and brush the dirt off my shorts. Jace stands, too. "I'm going to Rome," I say when my voice feels steady.

He looks at me, and I see the surprised flare of happiness in his expression. "The internship?"

"No," I say. "That's gone. But I've been accepted to the university there."

"That's so good, Emma. Really, really good."

"A change of scenery will help."

He smiles and something of his old self is there. "I'm going to turn down the Bergen. I'm not sure where I'll go or what I'm going to do. But for now I'm going to try and be a friend to Dillon."

I nod. I don't know what to say.

"One day I'd like to be a friend to you, too?" His voice rises on a question.

I look out over the hills, spotted with green and a few determined wildflowers. "Right now I need some time. I need some *Star Trek*." I choke on a half-laugh, half-sob. "But one day, maybe."

"Maybe is good. I can live with maybe."

And then, even though I shouldn't, I reach up and hug Jace. He hugs me back, hard. We stay like that for a long moment, the sound of his heart beating in my ear. Both of us holding on . . . and letting go. When I pull back, my eyes are wet again.

"Take care of yourself, Emma."

"I will," I say, and I smile because those words mean something. They mean everything. "You too."

Then I turn to face my future. In just a few months, I'm

going to *Italy*. I'm going to fly across an ocean and land in a new world full of discovery and adventure and *possibility*.

And I'm going to be okay. Better than okay. I'm going to make history.

I take my first step down the hill toward Rome.

AUGUST 25, AD 79

SECOND HOUR, 8:00 A.M.

In the tomb of the basement, Anna hears the ceaseless chanting of the gardener and the prayers of the housemaids. It's what she does not hear that makes her heart race. The fall of pumice and ash has slowed to a trickle.

She meets Marcus's eyes. "We must go. Now. This is our chance."

"The rock has stopped falling!" he exclaims. "We are safe!"

Anna shakes her head. "We will be buried alive if we do not go now."

Uncertainty flickers across his face. His eyes, which she once thought so beautiful, seem only weak. "Let us wait just a little while longer. To be certain."

Anna understands now that she has already waited far too long.

She gathers the help of the other slaves and together they push at the door. Rubble blocks it from the other side but they strain until a great crash comes from without and the door is shoved open inch by inch. Her heart pounds—but this time with hope.

Ash covers piles of rubble but the gardener is strong and with the help of the others, he fights a way aboveground.

It is not too late! She feels it. Hell is taking one final breath before unleashing itself.

"Anna!"

Marcus claws his way up behind her. "Wait!"

But she is done waiting.

"Anna!"

Broken plaster and shattered stone scrape her skin raw and still she presses forward. Inky black stretches above where the roof once was, but the rubble creates an uneven ground, solid enough to hold her weight. Every inch forward is a fight. The air is gone, consumed by smoke that blisters Anna's nose and throat. Her lungs burn. She will not die!

There—the street!

Shouts sound as others emerge from their hiding places. She pushes forward, sobbing with the will to live. Keep moving, keep moving!

She is only steps from the door when a sudden stillness falls like a blanket over the world. It is as if the very earth has paused.

"Anna!" Marcus tugs at her tunic. He does not understand, but she does.

She waited too long.

She yanks at the ring with her last breath, her last thought— wanting, needing—*to be free.*

When the blast hits, death comes so quickly Anna does not feel it.

*   *   *

Two thousand years have gone by and Anna is an ashen figure buried under fifteen feet of dirt. She lies under a part of Pompeii that has yet to be excavated.

But one day, it will be.

When archaeologists uncover her form, perfectly preserved in ash, they will find the figure of a man just behind her, reaching for her. They will find a ring upon her finger. And they will paint a tableau of love.

Only the truth will remain buried.

Author's Note

Books often come to me in bits and pieces, but this one started with the clear vision of a scene: Dillon and Emma around a campfire with their friends. It's a dark night, and the conversation is about graduation only a few months off and where they'll end up. Dillon, with his arms lovingly around Emma, says he'd die without her.

That scene never made it into the book, but I couldn't shake the idea of a boy who loved his girlfriend so passionately he couldn't live without her. There was a time when I would've thought that romantic. When I would have wished I had a boyfriend like Dillon.

But that was before I saw news stories about teens killing themselves over broken hearts. Before I read the love letter of a girl who was murdered by her boyfriend, who then killed himself. Before I saw images of young people who would never age because they had died carrying out suicide pacts.

All in the name of love.

And that got me thinking:

What does love look like?

What does abuse look like?

What happens when the lines blur?

As Emma says to herself at one point, how can love be bad? I'm the kind of person who's always believed in soul mates and Red Strings, so I like to believe that every relationship is a good one. But the frightening truth, according to DoSomething.org, is that one in three young people will be in an unsafe or unhealthy relationship.

One in three!

I knew this was a story I needed to tell.

I learned many things as I researched and wrote this book. I had numerous conversations with mental health professionals, including a clinical psychologist and two social workers, one of whom answered suicide hotlines and worked in teen rehab facilities. I learned that behavioral changes can often occur in the late teen years, especially in young men. I learned that mental illness is not so clear-cut that a therapist can point to a certain behavior and make a diagnosis. To do so would be like hearing someone cough and deciding whether it's a cold, the flu, or cancer. For that reason, I didn't put a label on Dillon's condition. But I like to believe he's going to be okay because he's getting the help he needs.

I also want to be clear that I'm not suggesting mental health issues are always the cause of abuse in relationships, or even a factor. This book is only meant to honestly reflect one relationship—that of Emma and Dillon.

Ultimately, this book is a love story. It's about a love worth *living* for—the love of yourself. As a therapist told me, one of the hardest things any person ever faces is putting their own needs above those of someone they love. It's hard, yes, but it's also okay. Please know this:

You matter.

You can't fix everything.

There is help available, and you are not a failure if you ask for it.

I encourage you to ask for help if you're in a relationship and feeling overwhelmed or scared, or if you think someone you care about needs help. One more important thing I learned by writing this book is that there are many wonderful, caring people out there who not only want to help, but *can*. Go online to find resources in your area. Most counties have crisis hotlines that respond right away. Or start with the links below.

Take care.

Amy

Resources

Adolescent Crisis Intervention & Counseling Nineline: 1-800-999-9999

DoSomething.org 1 in 3 of Us Campaign: dosomething.org /campaigns/1-3-us

Mental Health America (MHA): mentalhealthamerica.net

National Alliance on Mental Illness (NAMI): nami.org

National Domestic Violence Hotline/Love Is Respect: loveisrespect.org. Also offers free online chat, or call 1-866-331-9474.

National Suicide Prevention Lifeline: 1-800-273-TALK (8255)

Teen Mental Health: teenmentalhealth.org

Acknowledgments

Thank you to:

Dr. William Heywood, clinical psychologist, who spoke with me early on and whose experience and knowledge paved the way for this story. Barbara Kanal, Doctor of Social Work, who generously read an early manuscript, answered many questions over many months, and provided much needed insight into these characters. Judy Stock, Master of Social Work, for sharing her experiences working in support programs for teens. And LeAnn Dykstra, my nurse friend, for not hanging up on me when I called and said, "So, a guy comes into the hospital with a knife wound. . . ." I'm so grateful to every professional who gave valuable time to help me with this story. Any errors are entirely mine.

Critique partners and friends Terry Lynn Johnson for reading early versions, late versions, and panicked emails in between. Christina Mandelski for our mini-retreat in Austin and the quest for *Walking Dead* episodes. Bill Konigsberg and Erin Jade Lange for seeing the ending before I did. Gae Polisner, Kiki Hamilton, Nate Evans, Daphne Atkeson, the Writer Workshop group at The Writing Barn, and the *Graduates*—your Monday emails are lifesavers.

Caryn Wiseman, my agent, for also wearing the hats of editor, cheerleader, therapist, and friend. I can't imagine what I would do without you.

Krista Vitola, my editor, with whom I feel privileged to work. You asked all the right questions and pointed me in directions I wouldn't have thought to take. Because of you, this is a much better book. And the whole team at Delacorte Press for lending your talents to this story and for all the ways you support me.

Librarians, teachers, bloggers, readers, and my friends at Changing Hands Bookstore—for every lovely, positive, encouraging thing you say and write. In case you didn't know, it matters very much!

And most especially my family. Dad—your memory inspires me every day. Rachel, who read an early draft and whose enthusiasm gave me confidence—thank you, my beautiful daughter. My favorite son, Kyle, and of course, Jake. I would die for you . . . but I'm much happier that I get to live with you.

About the Author

AMY FELLNER DOMINY is a former advertising copy-writer, playwright, and hula-hoop champion. Her previous novels for tweens and teens include *A Matter of Heart; OyMG,* a Sydney Taylor Notable Book; and *Audition & Subtraction.* Amy lives with her husband and various pets in Phoenix. Visit her online at amydominy.com.

Continue reading for a sneak peek.

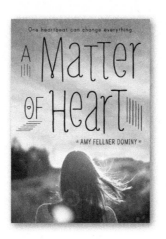

I can't breathe.

There's no time.

All around the pool, coaches yell and pace along the edge as if that'll make us swim faster. Parents shout out names. I don't hear which ones. In the water, it's a different kind of sound. The whoosh and thrum of the surface breaking over my cap. The churn of arms and the fizz of an exhale. The chant of *pull, pull* that I repeat in time with the *bmm bmm* of my heart.

Mostly, I just hear the scream of my burning lungs.

I don't listen.

In the last leg of a 100 free, there's no time for breathing. Not if you want to win.

Pull, pull.

Twenty-five yards left. That's it. Almost in reach. Everything I want is almost within reach.

Pull, pull.

Through the bubbles and froth I glimpse the rising beauty of the wall. I'm not breathing. Just pushing. Reaching.

Pull, pull—

My arm stretches, my fingertips search for the pebbly surface. There!

Yes!

I explode out of the water, my mouth wide as I gasp, dragging air into my clenched lungs.

I grab hold of the wall and turn toward the scoreboard. I rip off my goggles. My eyes, blurred and achy, stare. There's my name: *A. Lipman, lane 4.* Was it enough? Was *I* enough?

"Nice finish, Lipman!" It's Coach somewhere behind me, moving down the lanes. I hear him call to Alicia, another Horizon swimmer, in lane 6.

I drink the air and will the scoreboard to show the results I want. It took so much to get here. Months of two-a-day practices. Of pushing myself so hard there were mornings I couldn't lift my arms to wash my hair. All of it for one moment in time—literally. Fifty-eight seconds. Maybe fifty-seven.

The board flashes red. Times appear, along with finishing places.

Yes! First place, a school record, and my personal best— 57:56. Olympic qualifying time will be around 57:19.

My hand shoots up in a fist pump. Water splashes over my face and I blink my lashes clear as I smile because I don't have the air to laugh.

A shadow suddenly blocks the sun and I look up to see